"I told you years ago that the next time I kissed you it would be because you wanted me to."

He leisurely moved his gaze along her cheeks and over her nose, coming to rest on her mouth.

"Do you want to kiss me now, Paige?" he asked softly.

Her heart turned a crazy cartwheel in her chest, and she gasped. "Certainly not." She meant to look away, but instead she found herself staring back at him, mesmerized by the ready male awareness on his face. Her heart pounded in wild rhythm with the restless waves.

He released her to tuck a wayward piece of hair behind her ear. "You sure about that?"

Of course she was sure. He was the owner of the lewd resort. A man who strolled casually along his poolside where half-naked women threw themselves at him. He was wild...he was sexy...he was cocky...he was—she gulped—moving closer. Then he was lowering his head...and he was kissing her.

Dear Reader

It's hard to express the feeling of utter joy, seeing my dream come true with Harlequin Mills & Boon's publication of my first book, GETTING HOT IN HAWAII. I hope this novel sweeps you off to the Hawaiian Islands, a tropical oasis away from the troubles of daily life, to a paradise surrounded by lush palm trees, glistening ocean waves, and the brush of the island breeze.

Hawaii is my favourite vacation spot, where my husband and I spend our days hiking through vine-draped trails that twist through the foliage-covered jungles. And when we're not enjoying the tropical forests, we love to golf on the beautiful ocean-lined courses. Some of my best memories come from our times in Hawaii, and that's why I set my first novel on Kauai, the perfect place to fall in love.

I hope you enjoy this story of two high school chums who have shed the awkwardness of youth and find a second chance at love. When Paige Pipkin runs into her nerdy study partner years later, he looks a little different than she remembers. Same voice, *much* different package. Jack Banta is now hot, charming, and the perfect touch of naughty! The first time she kissed him it was because she had to—for try-outs in the school play. But he promises that the second time she kisses him...it will be because she *wants* to. Join Paige as she takes a leap into the unknown, a leap towards possibility...a leap for love.

Happy reading!

Kerri LeRoy

GETTING HOT IN HAWAII

BY
KERRI LEROY

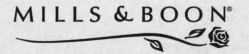

MILLS & BOON®

First published in Great Britain 2006
Harlequin Mills & Boon Limited,
Eton House, 18-24 Paradise Road, Richmond, Surrey TW9 1SR

© Kerri LeRoy 2006

Standard ISBN 0 263 84993 7
Promotional ISBN 0 263 85120 6

Set in Times Roman 10½ on 13¼ pt.
171-0706-51824

Printed and bound in Spain
by Litografia Rosés S.A., Barcelona

GETTING HOT
IN HAWAII

Dedicated to my beloved husband—my love, my life. And with deep gratitude to a wonderful editor, Brenda Chin. Special thanks to my critique partners and dear friends, Cindy Nielsen and Tiffinie Helmer, for all the hard work and all the laughs. And many thanks to the Wasatch Mountain Fiction Writers.

CHAPTER ONE

"HEY! What'd you do that for?" Paige Pipkin twisted in her chair and tried to retrieve her papers from Aunt Naomi's grasp, but her wacky aunt made a perfect pirouette out of her reach. She came to a stop next to Paige's seat at the kitchen table and skimmed through the pages.

"What is this, anyway?" Aunt Naomi pushed a frizzy, salon-orange lock of curls off her forehead and squinted at the paperwork.

"It's an application for my next doctorate at Stanford. Now, give it here." Paige grabbed her precious forms and carefully smoothed them out on the table.

Before Paige could stop her, Aunt Naomi snatched them away again and perused the top of the first page. "What degree are you going for this time?"

"Ancient History and Mediterranean Archaeology." Paige snapped her fingers at her, motioning for a return. "I'll have to acquire command of two ancient languages and obtain practical archaeological experience. Doesn't that sound intriguing?"

"Hmmph." Aunt Naomi sniffed and ripped the application form in two.

"Hey!" Paige stared at her in disbelief.

Aunt Naomi handed the pieces back and smiled calmly. "Relax, dear." She reached into the folds of her flowing, multi-colored floral blouse and winked. "I have something far better than that." She pulled out a glossy brochure and plunked it on the smooth oak table. "Now *that's* what I call intriguing."

Still miffed, Paige frowned down at the bright brochure. What was Naomi up to this time? "Club Lealea, Kauai's Hottest Singles' Resort." She peered over the top of her glasses at her aunt, who had taken the chair across from her. "What?" Paige said. "You're going to a singles' club?" No big shocker there.

"No, *I'm* not going to a singles' club. *You* are."

"Huh?" Paige squinted at the photo on the front of the pamphlet. Palm trees, a swim-up bar, women in bikinis, men with six-pack abs. *Please.* She slid the brochure across the table toward her aunt and chuckled. "I'm *so* not going to that place. But you have a nice time." She aligned each half of her college application back together and wondered where the Scotch tape was.

"Not so fast," Aunt Naomi said. "I told you, I'm not going. But you should. You could use a break from the university. I mean, think about it, Paige. You already have a doctorate in Romance Languages, and now this? Another degree? In…in…what was it again? Boring History and Whatdyacallit Archaeology?"

Paige couldn't stop a half-laugh from escaping. "It's Ancient History and Mediterranean Archaeology."

"Okay. What you said. But still, what are you going to do with that degree?"

"I don't know. Teach some day? I love learning new things."

"Yes, I know, and I love that about you, honey. You're my bright, intelligent niece, and I wouldn't change one brilliant hair on your head. But honestly, Paige, you need to get out from behind your textbooks and experience life." Aunt Naomi picked up the brochure and waggled it. "Live a little. Shake things up a bit." Her aunt flicked past the first page of the resort flyer and ran her eyes down the second. "Use the vacation to figure out what you want to do with the rest of your life." She turned a third page. "Think about getting a real job, outside the university. Learn some social skills." She turned another page. "Mmm, yes. Hello, Handsome." She held up a photo of one of the single men at the club and wiggled her eyebrows at Paige. "Maybe get *laid*."

Paige gasped.

"What? I meant as in flowers. You know, lei-ed. It's Hawaii, after all."

"Uh-huh." Paige rolled her eyes.

"You could meet someone special," her aunt continued. "Like *him*." She held up another photo and in a sing-song tone added, "Someone I know isn't getting any young-er."

Paige shook her head.

The guy in the photo looked bronzed and muscular,

lifting weights in the club's gym. Yes, he was hot. But please. A meat market singles' resort? She didn't think so.

She would never fit in at a place like that. The mere thought made her break out into a sweat. She rubbed her palms along her jeans and studied the bikini-clad women on the front of the brochure. Paige was all about shirts that buttoned to the throat. About books and dissertations. She was a *scholar*. "I like my life just fine," she said, disliking the hollow sound of her voice. She cleared her throat. "Besides, a new semester's just about to start. I've been looking forward to it." She broke eye contact with her aunt and glanced down at her torn application.

Aunt Naomi had a point. Paige had just turned twenty-eight and she still hadn't met that special someone yet. And some day, she'd like to. But how? Life was much safer in the seclusion of her books. She shuddered at the thought of being out there in the singles' scene. She felt awkward in social situations. How had Naomi put it? Being out there, shaking things up? Good grief. Not to mention getting *laid?*

She coughed. "A singles' resort just isn't my…my style."

"Well, maybe it's time to try on a new style." Naomi gave her a smug look.

Paige froze. Oh, no. She knew that look. "What is that?" she asked. "That—" she made a circular motion "—that look?"

"What look? There's no look."

Her aunt's feigned innocence wasn't fooling Paige. "Aunt Naomi, what have you done?"

"Hmm?" Naomi glanced at her fingers, as if engrossed in inspecting her sparkly purple nail polish. "I just think it's time for you to leave the nest." She sighed and returned her hands to her lap. She leveled her gaze directly at Paige. "Look, I made you a three-week reservation at Club Lealea." She shrugged. "Your bags are packed. You leave tomorrow. It's already paid for."

"What?" Paige pushed back her chair. Its legs added their own protest against the hardwood floor. "You shouldn't have done that." She rose and paced the length of the kitchen. "What did you do, dip into your life savings? You can't afford to pay for a trip like this." She returned to the table. "You're crazy."

"Hmmph. I'm the crazy aunt you love." Naomi rose and put her arm around Paige, a wide grin bridging her bright, powdered cheeks.

Paige sighed. This was not happening.

"Oh, come on, Paige. Who would turn down a vacation like this? You're the one who's crazy."

Not when she considered the expense. Besides, three weeks? That was such a long time. Her mind spun considering all the aspects of a trip like that. She'd be by herself. She'd have to socialize, meet new people, maybe even go on a date. What about her classes at the college? The whole idea made her feel sick. Dizzy, she sank back into her seat and stared up at Aunt Naomi's well-meaning expression.

Her aunt had always been there for her. She'd taken her in every time her busy parents had dumped Paige on Naomi. As research scientists, her parents had always been off on one assignment or another. But her aunt had always been there with a big hug. She'd never made Paige feel like an imposition. She'd been there with her free-spirited smile, her trips to the ice-cream shop and the opportunity to play dress-up with her large, jangly jewelry. Later, she'd listened to Paige's teenage woes, offered make-up tips and given advice about boys. Not that there'd been many guys in Paige's past. But nonetheless…

She looked back at the aunt who stood next to her chair, watching her closely. At the one person who knew her better than anyone.

Aunt Naomi, who had never married, had retired from teaching junior high in Kauai right at the same time Paige had been ready for college. Nervous to go out on her own, Paige had invited Naomi to accompany her to California while she attended Stanford. True to form, her dear aunt and confidante had gladly joined Paige in California, allowing her to live rent-free in the house she'd purchased while Paige attended school. But one degree had led to the next, until now…

Paige smiled ruefully at her aunt. She owed her. Big time. She could never repay the kindness and sacrifice this woman had shown her through the years. And she could tell her aunt felt strongly about the trip. Heck, she'd already packed Paige's bags.

She sighed. She supposed she could refuse. But then, Naomi might do something even more drastic—like toss her out of the house, forcing her to get a life once and for all. Paige didn't think her aunt would go to those lengths, but still…

"Are you sure this is a good idea?" she asked.

Aunt Naomi nodded, her long, dangly half-moon earrings flapping in earnest against her throat. She met Paige's eyes, and her gaze grew serious for a moment. "Listen, honey. I don't want you to end up old and alone like me."

Paige frowned. "But you're happy, right? You've always said you had no regrets." Suddenly, she wondered if, deep down, her dear, sweet aunt had been unhappy all along. "Is that not true?"

"No, no, I've been happy. But I was lucky." Aunt Naomi smiled at her softly. "I've always had you." She reached down and played with Paige's pony-tail, smoothing it affectionately as she'd always done. "You've been the daughter I never had."

Paige gulped, trying to calm the rush of emotion that suddenly clogged her throat. How could she say no to this trip when it clearly meant so much to her aunt? "Do you want to come with me? I'm sure there'll be some older men—"

"I knew you'd say that." Aunt Naomi chuckled. "You need to do this on your own. It'll be good for you. Get some sun. *Meet* people. You'll be fine. I figure this place is just about perfect. Not only is it the hottest new singles' resort in the country, but it will also be familiar, since you spent two years of high school in Kauai." Her eyebrows rose with renewed enthusiasm. "And guess what?"

Paige was afraid to ask.

"Do you remember Irene Nielsen? She still lives there, and she's been asking me to go visit. I'm thinking of flying over for a few days during your stay to visit her. I can pop by to see how you're doing. Sound good?"

Actually, it did. Paige nodded. "I don't see what good a three-week stint at a singles' club is going to do for me, though. What if I return and still want to pursue that archaeology degree?"

"Well, that would be fine," Aunt Naomi said. "All I'm asking is that you give it a try. Use the time to really think about your life and the direction you want it to take. If you come back and still want to go to school, then, who am I to stop you?" The twinkle returned to her eyes, and she picked the brochure up again. "But I'll bet you return from this place a new woman."

Paige smothered a snort. She doubted it. She looked at the pamphlet in her aunt's hands. Actually, it did look kind of fun. Tropical flowers, swimming pools, a resort environment. A big difference from the university library.

And even though she typically retreated to the comfort of her textbooks, she'd always secretly yearned to fit in. Ever since she was a young girl. Maybe it was time to give it a try. Join the fun for once in her life. Paige toyed with the college application on the table, running her fingertip along the rough, ripped edge. She'd always been smart enough. But was she brave enough? She watched Aunt Naomi flip through the brochure, studying the club's map and layout.

Paige supposed she could give it a try. It would make her aunt happy. Maybe she could look at the three-week vacation like a class assignment. An assignment to study the "native singles" and learn how to fit in. The idea grew in her mind, and soon she began to feel a semblance of hope taking shape. That was right. She could read articles, couldn't she? Read the latest magazines about dating, about resort vacations. Check out a book or two on socializing, how to make polite chit-chat. If she was going to do this, she might as well do it right. She could tackle it like any other class she'd taken. It was the only way she knew.

"Mmm-mmm," Naomi said, interrupting her thoughts. She held up the back page of the flyer, showing a picture of a surfer grasping his surfboard on his way to ride waves. "I'd like to grasp *his* board, if you know what I mean."

Paige groaned. Even the houseplants knew what she meant.

Aunt Naomi lovingly ran her fingertip over the young man's biceps and then began hula dancing around the kitchen table. "Tell him 'aloha' for me when you get there." She hula-bumped her hip against Paige's chair, almost knocking her out of her seat.

Paige righted herself, giving Aunt Naomi a half-hearted smile. "You got it," she mumbled. "One 'aloha' to the surfer guy." She lowered her head to the table. *Alo-freakin'-ha.*

Club Lealea's shuttle bus pulled into the front gates of the lush resort. Towering palm trees flanked the entry. Paige gazed out the window at the tropical greenery that swayed with the breeze as if beckoning her.

She was the only passenger on the bus, and she'd

enjoyed the sunset ride along the twisting jungle-lined road to the club.

"Welcome to Lealea." The bus driver pulled to the front of the massive resort, and the hiss of the opening doors pierced the early evening air. He rose and plucked her suitcase off the rack, carrying it down the steps for her. "I'll give this to the bellboy."

She followed him out of the air-conditioned shuttle and stepped into the hot, humid Hawaiian breeze.

"Don't worry about my bag," she said. "I'll take it from here." Aunt Naomi had lent Paige her suitcase—an old throwback to the seventies—and Paige had crossed her fingers that the ancient luggage would make the flight in one piece.

"You sure you want to carry this yourself? It's pretty heavy," the driver said, holding it up and glancing at the oversized daisy sticker pasted on the side.

Paige nodded and handed him a tip. She didn't dare let anyone take her luggage. The last thing she wanted was for the bag to be thrown around. Its rickety snaps looked ready to fall apart any minute.

The bus driver shrugged, thanked her and reentered the bus, angling the weighty vehicle away from the curb.

Paige adjusted her grip on her suitcase and gazed up at the sprawling singles' club before her. She knew her sudden queasiness had nothing to do with the winding road she'd just traveled. She took a deep breath and moved forward.

Elegant was the first word that came to mind as she gazed at the palatial resort.

Just then, a chicken flapped its way out of a bush and ran across her path. She shook her head. She'd forgotten about all the chickens on Kauai. Elegant or not, the resort couldn't escape the free-range chickens that inhabited the small island. With an absence of predators for the feral birds, Kauai natives had grown used them. They were everywhere. Just another part of living on The Garden Island.

She headed up the stairs to the beautiful resort, its balconies and walkways dripping with island flora. A tropical oasis away from the troubles of daily life. A thrill of excitement scurried up her spine, along with a tinge of apprehension. Could she really do this? Alone? The fresh scent of hibiscus and plumeria drifted upon the winds, cooling the perspiration beneath her ponytail at the back of her neck.

On the flight over, she'd finished her copy of *Cocktail Parties: A Shrinking Violet's Handbook to Becoming the BlueBelle of the Ball*. She sighed and wondered if she could make practical use of the tips she'd learned. It was only three weeks, right? With a deep breath, she made her way up the wide stone staircase to the entrance of the club.

On the landing, the revolving doors opened, and a young, bare-chested man, linked arm in arm with two women in coconut bikini tops and grass skirts, stumbled through the door. The threesome bumped smack into Paige at the top of the steps.

"Oops. Sorry, babe." The guy gave her a quick once-over and grinned. "Wanna join us?"

"Uh, no, thanks."

He lifted a shoulder. "All right. Come on, ladies." He took a swig from his beer bottle and let out a loud, drunken holler. Then he draped his arm over his "ladies", and the threesome staggered down the steps.

Nice. Paige's queasiness turned into actual nausea, and she wondered again what Aunt Naomi had gotten her into. She entered the club and glanced around the lobby. A magnificent waterfall statue of a nude man and woman adorned the foyer. The man held up a conch shell, cascading water over the woman who stood before him in a sensual pose. A fitting statue for a singles' resort.

She gulped, feeling out of place.

A man in his mid-twenties sauntered by, biceps bulging, wearing nothing but a pair of shorts that settled low on his hips. He looked casual and carefree, a towel slung over one shoulder, his hair a sexy blond wave. He spared Paige a sidelong glance and grinned.

Be sure to make eye contact and smile. That was what her book had said. She returned his grin with a shaky smile of her own, but he'd already turned to watch a girl in a hot pink bikini strut past.

Paige dropped her ridiculous grin and shifted her bag to her other hand. Oka-a-a-ay. So, she'd failed that pop quiz. But at least she'd known the answer. Her failure had been in the delivery. Maybe it was time to buy a hot pink bikini? She grimaced at the thought and headed for check-in.

Jack Banta sat behind his desk at Club Lealea and smiled patiently at the salesgirl seated across from him.

She couldn't be more than sixteen or seventeen. Working her first summer job, no doubt, hawking flowered leis door-to-door. God, what a chore that must be, lugging that huge box of flowers in and out of office buildings all day long.

She twisted her chubby fingers in her lap and re-hearsed her stilted sales pitch. "The leis of Old Hawaii were a symbol of love," she said. "The circle of a lei is symbolic for the circle of an embrace. Perfect for a singles' club where people are searching for love." She shifted in her seat, her cheeks flushed.

Jack had to hand it to her. She'd tailored her pitch to his business. Not bad. He nodded to let her know he was following.

She cleared her throat and continued on.

Jack half listened to the teenager, recalling the awk-wardness of youth. He'd had a real time of it himself— being a small, skinny kid. His growth spurt hadn't occurred until his first year of college, but, hell, better late than never.

He felt for the young salesgirl sitting across from him. He really did. But he didn't need any more flowers for the club. He'd been receiving a great discount from his buddy, a local grower. He glanced beside his desk at the box of hibiscus that had just arrived yesterday. His housekeeping staff left a flower on each guest's pillow daily.

"Why not hand out leis to your guests at check-in?" the girl continued. "Right when their search for love is beginning."

He smiled. Not a bad idea. "What's your quota for the week?" he asked, interrupting her spiel.

"Um, I'm supposed to sell five full boxes this week."

"That's a lot of flowers to carry around."

"Tell me about it," she said, clearly forgetting her professional sales pitch for a second. "I've been lugging these things around all day, and I haven't sold one of them yet. And the day's almost over. Not to mention how hot it is out there." She flapped the front of her shirt against her chest to cool off. "Luckily, they've given me a refrigerated van to drive the flowers around in. But I still have to carry them into every building." She stopped, as if she'd just remembered her reason for being there. "But, um, it's not so bad. I love leis," she ended sheepishly. "They're pretty, and they smell great. Here, smell." She held a yellow lei out to him.

"Uh, yes. Nice."

"So, how many may I write you up for?" she asked.

Oh, smooth. Going for the ol' assumptive close. The girl had guts.

She hesitated when he didn't answer right away. "Only if you want some, that is," she said.

He didn't. "I do." What the hell? He didn't have the heart to turn her down. "I'll take five."

"Great!" She pulled five single leis out of her enormous box and set them carefully across his desk.

"No. I mean, I'll take five boxes."

"*Really?*" She stared at him, her mouth open. "That's a whole week's worth!" She sat there, clearly stunned.

Sure, why not? His resort could always use some

extra leis. "Why don't I get someone to help you bring them in?" He rose and held out his hand.

When they shook hands, she blushed, then quickly glanced away, smothering a nervous giggle.

Jack was used to that reaction from women—the subtle and sometimes not-so-subtle glint of female appreciation when they first met him.

At that moment, Lulu, his activities coordinator, stuck her head through his office doorway, her long black braid swinging. "Excuse me, Jack. Nick's on the phone. Line three. He wants to discuss next week's schedule."

"Tell him I'll be right there. And can you get one of the bellboys to help this young lady carry her flowers in? I bought five boxes."

"Five boxes!" Lulu frowned, her face growing red beneath her native Hawaiian Islander tan. "Where are we going to put five boxes of flowers?"

"I don't know," Jack said. "Why don't you put one box at the front desk and leave the rest in here for now?"

The salesgirl, obviously feeling more confident than when she'd first walked in, chimed in eagerly. "I'll help you make room."

He chuckled. He bet she would. He picked up a red hibiscus from his local grower's box and gently tucked it behind her ear. "Every pretty saleswoman should have a flower for her hair."

Her smile widened. "Thanks, Mr Banta."

"It's Jack."

"Jack. And thanks for the order, too."

He nodded, happy to make her day. She reminded

him of himself as a teen—introverted, shy. "You're very welcome. Good luck with your job." He winked. "Maybe your boss will give you the rest of the week off now." He turned to Lulu. "Can you fill in whatever paperwork is required here, while I talk to Nick?"

"Sure." Lulu ushered the girl from his office.

Jack followed them out to check on the lobby before he answered Nick's call. He strode the few steps to the check-in counter and surveyed the scene. Everything seemed to be running smoothly. The resort bustled with singles walking to and from the pool, while others chatted in groups. Nothing out of the ordinary.

He picked up a phone behind the counter and punched line three. "Hey, Nick. What's up?" His assistant manager's voice came on the line, asking about the following week's schedule. "A poolside limbo contest on Thursday?" Nick hadn't failed him yet with his entertainment plans for the club. Jack nodded. "Yeah, okay, that'll work." He switched the phone to his other ear. "Any ideas for Friday?"

He watched a cute visitor with a black pony-tail lug an odd-looking suitcase across the elegant white marble floor. Was that a daisy on her bag? The large flower, reminiscent of hippies and free love, seemed inconsistent with the image the young woman presented.

She looked like the straitlaced type, but it was always the bookish ones that did it for Jack.

He liked her prim, pursed lips as she scoped out the scene, the almost imperceptible lift of her head as she glanced at the half-naked bodies that strutted through his hotel lobby. Her prude manner wasn't lost on him, and he was suddenly piqued by a desire to join her in whatever adventure she expected to find at Club Lealea. Wondering what brought her to his place, he took one last look at her and returned his attention to his assistant manager on the phone.

"Look, Nick, how many bikini contests can we hold in one month before it gets old? How about a men's swimsuit contest for the ladies this time?" Jack listened to Nick and nodded. "All right. See you when you get here." He hung up the phone.

Lulu rounded the front counter and squatted to look in a drawer. "Have you seen my pen anywhere?" she asked. "The one with my name engraved on it? The one you always seem to borrow and never return? I need to sign for your flowers."

"Nope. Haven't seen it." He grabbed a message pad and scribbled a note to himself.

Lulu took a pen off the counter and headed outside to sign off on the leis.

When Jack finished his note, he looked for the cute visitor he'd been watching a moment ago.

Where had she gone?

He leaned over the top of the counter and craned his neck to the side. Aha. She was at the brochure rack off to the left, sifting through the club's travel and tour pamphlets.

"Hi, Jack."

A female voice interrupted his study, and he settled himself back behind the counter. The greeting had come

from a redhead approaching the front desk. He straightened his shirt and donned his charming resort-host
smile. "Ah, the lovely Miss Cindy."

She wore a clingy, low-cut black dress that molded
to her bosomy figure. She was a fairly new arrival.
Where was she from again? Oh, yeah, Arizona.

He gave an impressed whistle under his breath for
her benefit and shook his head. "Arizona's loss is
Hawaii's gain. How's the most sought-after woman at
our club doing?"

She beamed beneath his compliment. "I'm doing ter-
rific—" she paused, then added in a sultry voice "—now."
She leaned into the counter, her creamy breasts practically
pouring onto the marble top before him.

Wow. Hello. He wondered how she expected a guy
to react to that. He supposed he could start clapping.

Instead, he politely averted his gaze. At the moment,
the only thing on his mind was keeping the front desk
clear for the visitor at the brochure rack—the prissy-
looking one with her nose buried in a tour guide. Surely
she'd come over to check in any minute.

"So, Cindy," he said. "It's supposed to rain tonight.
Did you hear we moved the luau indoors to the Tiki
Lounge? Starts soon. I know a couple of the guys were
hoping you'd show up."

"Really? That sounds good. I'm starving." Her
gaze said she'd prefer Jack as her main dish. "Will
you be there?"

He tilted his head and tried to look disappointed.
"Nah. Gotta work."

She straightened from the counter. "Maybe next time?"

"You're on." Jack watched her walk away. He was the first person most of the guests met, and too often women targeted him as their vacation date of choice. But he wanted repeat customers, and getting involved in messy relationships wouldn't achieve that goal. As a rule, he avoided attachments, opting for simple, harmless flirting. That was what kept most of his clients happy. He craned his neck to get another look at the pretty newcomer still standing at the brochure rack.

Mmm-mmm. Then again, some rules were meant to be broken… The object of his attention held a pamphlet close to her face and squinted at it carefully. Then she reached into the pocket of her olive-green shorts and took out a pair of glasses for a closer look.

Nice touch. He loved a woman in glasses. Now if only that long black pony-tail were pulled into a strict little bun—the kind he'd love to uncoil through his fingers or, better yet, shake loose during a romp of passion. Her slender black glasses looked stern, academic…and sexy in a curious way. The bridge of her nose wrinkled as she concentrated, and suddenly it struck him as oddly familiar.

My God. It was Paige. Paige Pipkin.

He'd heard she'd left Kauai after high school and never looked back, moving to the mainland to earn her doctorate.

Now, here she was. Memories of the girl he'd known in high school flooded back. He'd longed for her with the secret crush of an awkward teen—a longing never satisfied and never *ever* forgotten.

The bustling sounds of the club faded into the background. Jack swallowed, and for an instant he felt like the shy, awkward kid who had done the same thing he was doing now—watching Paige Pipkin from afar.

He jerked himself upright. What the hell was he doing? He wasn't the same school kid any more. He was Jack Banta—successful resort owner, eligible bachelor, and, damn it, some might even call him a playboy. He shrugged. If the title fit...

His eyes narrowed slightly as he watched Paige. Yep, she'd shot him down for dates repeatedly. Each time he'd mustered the nerve to ask her out, thinking she would finally agree, she'd turned him down again.

As he watched her a thought slowly formed in his mind. How would it feel to give her a little taste of what she'd passed up in school? Wasn't that every nerd's dream? To surface years later, rich and handsome, and steal the heart of the girl who got away?

The new Jack knew what made women tick...as well as what made them sigh with pleasure. And he'd love nothing more than to seduce the stern, academic glasses right off the strait-laced Paige Pipkin. Maybe his opportunity had just walked through the door. To have Paige in his arms, staring up at him, a sexy invitation on her lips...

The more he thought about it, the more the idea took hold, warming him with a satisfaction he hadn't felt for quite some time.

How long would she be here? Two weeks? Three? That was all he'd need. A slow smile played across his mouth. He might have missed his chance with her in school, but he sure as hell wasn't going to let it slip by a second time. By the end of her stay at Club Lealea, she'd be leaving…wanting more. Call it a sensual payback of sorts.

Paige raised her gaze from the brochure rack and glanced toward his station at the front desk.

Jack quickly leaned away from the counter and smoothed his shirt across his chest. As she approached his check-in area, he muttered beneath his breath, "Yep. Time for a little payback." He grinned to himself.

Lulu walked out of his office with a box of leis in her arms. She plunked the flowers behind the front desk. "What's that about paybacks?" she asked.

"Hmm? Oh, nothing."

She glanced in Paige's direction and frowned, then shrugged. "By the way, I found my pen in your office." She wiggled it at him with a playful smile. "Someone can't keep his hands off my things." She gave him a light-hearted smack on the arm and circled around the counter. "It's past quitting time. Are you about done here?"

"Not yet." He wasn't leaving until he'd had a chance to talk to Paige. He watched Lulu swirl her finger in a circle on the marble countertop, tracing its pattern.

"You know, I'm making a seafood dish tonight," she said. "Native to the islands. Handed down through my family for generations." She stopped following the pattern and looked at him, eyebrows raised. "I wouldn't mind some company."

"Oh, ah, thanks," Jack said. "But I'm working late tonight. I just talked to Nick, though. He's on his way over right now to pick up some paperwork. He might be up for it. I can have him call you at home if you want."

"Oh. Yeah. Well, whatever," she murmured. She pushed off the counter. "Guess I'll see you tomorrow."

"Bright and early." Jack smiled at her. She'd been a good employee, so far—always helpful when needed, always friendly. His brows lowered a fraction. Sometimes she seemed a little too friendly, almost...well, flirty. He shook his head. Nah. It must be his imagination. She knew better than that. They worked together.

Lulu grabbed her purse and left. Just in time, too. The front desk was finally free, and Paige was three steps away.

Jack resumed his position behind the counter and prepared himself to be reacquainted with the girl of his fantasies.

Suddenly, a young woman darted through the lobby, screaming with laughter, her grass skirt a rustling blur about her legs.

Her pursuer followed hot on her heels, a Super Soaker squirt gun in his hands. As he ran past he bumped into Paige, smacking against her suitcase and sending it skating across the floor. It tumbled once and fell open, scattering its contents in disarray.

The young guest paused to help, but Jack waved him away. "Go on after her. I can help here."

The guy grinned and took off after the girl.

Jack came out from behind the desk and knelt next to Paige. "Here, let me help." He handed a blouse to her that had fallen out of her bag and reached over to grab a hairbrush.

"That's okay," she murmured, grabbing items and shoving them into her bag. "I can manage."

He stared at the top of her head as she scooped up her belongings. Academics had been the only way he'd known how to connect with her in school. Thanks to that, she'd seen him as competition rather than a prospective date. They'd ended up going against each other for valedictorian. And he had beaten her out of the title, just barely. She had been crestfallen...and a bit angry, if he remembered correctly.

He reached over and pulled another pile of clothing closer to her bag. Frowning, he lifted a sizable mound of white cotton off the top. What in the hell...? *Oh*, it was panties. He cocked his head. Panties that could only be described as...geriatric.

Paige glanced up and snatched her underwear from the curve of his forefinger. "Do you mind?" She gave him a reproachful look.

She didn't recognize him.

He wasn't surprised. He no longer wore glasses. Besides, he was taller, now, and in great shape.

Jack smiled at Paige softly, feeling bad for her. This hadn't been a grand entrance. Certainly not what she'd expected for her resort experience, so far. He watched as she darted another look his way.

And then...there it was. The glint of sexual interest sparking through her gaze. The heated look...the soft blush.

She glanced away quickly, but he'd already seen it. He'd become accustomed to that reaction, and it gave him great pleasure to see it coming from *her*.

His sense of satisfaction grew, and he smiled to himself. Yep, it seemed his payback plan had just officially been set into motion.

Paige was still stuffing socks and shorts into her bag.

Jack picked up a wrinkled magazine off the floor and handed it back to her.

"Thanks," she mumbled. She paused and looked at him. "What was with those two anyway? Squirt guns? Clearly they'd been drinking. Aren't there rules about public intoxication at this resort?"

"Rules? Nah. What fun would that be?"

"Does the manager feel the same way?"

"I'd have to say he does. Since I'm the manager."

She snorted and went back to work on her luggage.

Jack took the opportunity to study her. Her shirt buttoned all the way to her throat…properly. Just like the Paige he remembered. But there was nothing proper about the way the fabric clung to her rounded breasts. Naughty really, but, oh, so nice.

Paige had filled out over the years, a tempting blend of hills and valleys he didn't remember, and Jack decided he liked the end result. He rose and grabbed a stapled magazine article that had landed at the base of the counter. He held the glossy pages out to her, glancing at the title. His grip tightened when he read the subject.

"A Woman's Guide to Making It, Not Faking It."

He leaned in and read the article closer. *Good Lord*.

He read out loud. "Ten ways to better orgasms?" He swallowed and gave her a second look. Maybe Paige *had* changed a bit since school. "I commend you. Sounds like you have high expectations for this trip." His lips twitched, and he gave her a wink. "Good luck."

CHAPTER TWO

PAIGE gasped and tugged at the magazine in the hotel manager's hand. He let go, and she fell backwards, landing on the chilly marble of the club's lobby.

What was he talking about?

She glanced down at the pages and frowned. "A Woman's Guide to Making It—" Aunt Naomi! Paige squeezed her eyes shut, heat spilling over her cheeks. She was going to kill her aunt. She must've put that in her bag.

Paige took a calming breath and opened her eyes. She shoved the magazine inside her suitcase and banged it shut, clicking the old metal snaps into place. Then she aimed a cool stare at the shameless man in front of her, his face the picture of good-natured amusement. "Thanks for the help. I'm ready to check in now." With as much dignity as she could muster, she rose and proceeded to the counter. His chuckle echoed behind her.

"Paige, you don't remember me, do you?"

She jerked her gaze back to him. How did he know her name?

He leaned one hand against the marble countertop and looked down at her with an easy grin.

"Have we met?"

"Sure have," he said. "I thought you were the cutest brainiac at Kauai High. But you were too busy trying to build a better science project than mine or taking first place on the debate team. I'll never forget your winning speech—'Staking out a Woman's Place in a Patriarchal Society'. How did that work out for you?"

Paige stared back at his teasing blue eyes. Then her mouth fell open. "Jackson Banta?"

She watched him pretend to glance around, making sure no one was listening. "I go by Jack these days," he said with a grin. "Jackson's kinda stuffy, don't you think?"

She gaped at the handsome man before her. *Jackson Banta?*

He looked so...so...different. He was, well...so *not* how he used to be. Same guy, *much* different package. He was tall and muscular in his khaki pants and white cotton shirt. Strong jaw. Chiseled cheekbones. And when he smiled his sensual lips and sandy blond hair, the color of warm caramel, added to his appeal. This man was self-assured, cocky almost. Not the quiet, studious guy she'd once known...and she wasn't sure she liked it. There was something disconcerting about him, about the way he looked at her. It made her feel self-conscious and in an oddly thrilling way...off-kilter.

Jackson Banta, once a nerd extraordinaire, was now definitely out of her league.

She absently fingered the top button of her shirt as if checking to see that it was still buttoned.

"So, what brings you back to Kauai, Paige?" His eyes traveled along her face, unhurried, interested.

How should she answer that? She didn't want to tell him her aunt had pushed her out of the nest. To "get laid" as she'd put it. Not that Paige had any plans to do *that*. She was here to…well… "I'm here for a little vacation," she said. "Just a break between studies." That was pretty much true.

"A break from studies, hmm? So, what are you studying these days?" He had the air of a man who could size up a person in a matter of seconds.

She fought the impulse to smooth back her hair. "I just finished a doctorate in Romance Languages at Stanford—" she glanced toward the hotel entrance and shifted her stance "—and I'm getting ready to study ancient history, with an emphasis on Mediterranean archaeology."

He simply nodded, his eyes still searching her face. They stared at each other in charged silence, until he broke the connection and glanced at his watch. "Well, we should get you checked in, shouldn't we?" He walked behind the counter and typed her name into the computer.

"So," Paige said. "You manage this place?"

"Not just manage it." He winked. "I *own* it."

Who'd have guessed that Jackson would become the owner of a sexy singles' resort? She shook her head and studied him. His light blue eyes narrowed as he concentrated on the computer screen, and the muscles in his forearm flexed with each tap of the keyboard.

God, he was gorgeous.

She paused. What was wrong with her? This was Jackson Banta, for heaven's sake. But that knowledge didn't stop her heart from jumping when he raised his gaze to hers.

"Your reservation says you're here for three weeks, then?"

"Yes. And, um, about that, uh, article you saw." Her cheeks heated all over again. "My aunt put that in there when I wasn't looking. She's—" How should she put it? "She's like that." Paige hated to mention the article again, but she really wanted him to know it wasn't her idea.

"Ah. The old my-aunt-put-that-in-my-bag excuse. I haven't heard that one in a while." He lifted a shoulder. "It's a singles' resort. You clearly came here to meet other singles while on vacation. Believe me, I've seen it all." He leaned forward and whispered, "Don't worry. Your secret's safe with me." Amusement flickered in his eyes.

He obviously found the article funny. She should just drop it. Trying to convince him would only make her look more foolish. She crossed her arms.

"Okay, you're all set," he said, handing a room key to her.

"Thanks." She turned to walk away, then stopped. "Jackson, what do you think about this hiking tour along the Na Pali coast?" She showed him the brochure she'd found when she'd first entered the club. "It leaves tomorrow morning."

He nodded. "Yep, that's a good one. In fact, all of our programs are fun. Lulu, our activities coordinator, looks after all of that stuff. She'll be here first thing in the morning. Her desk is right over there." He pointed across the lobby.

"Great. I'll sign up tomorrow."

"Our club's activities are a good way to meet people," Jack said.

"That's what I figured. The hula lessons look interesting, too. And maybe the on-site exercise program."

"Sounds like you have your schedule already filled."

She picked up her suitcase. "That's my plan."

"It's good to see you again, Paige," he said softly.

It was good to see him again, too. She swallowed. Maybe a little too good.

He reached down beneath the desk and came up with a light yellow lei in his hand. "Welcome to Lealea."

"Oh, thanks." She looped the fragrant string of flowers around her neck.

"By the way, we have bellboys here." He nodded at her suitcase. "You don't have to carry that thing by yourself." Raising his hand, he motioned to a group of bellboys across the lobby.

"No, that's okay," Paige said, but it was too late. A young, sexy-looking bellboy was already on his way over. She glanced at Jackson. "This bag is old. I don't want it falling open again. I'll carry it myself."

The bellboy arrived at the desk, muscles bulging

beneath his short-sleeved uniform, a helpful grin on his face. "I'll take that for you, ma'am." He reached for the suitcase in her hand.

"No. Please." She smiled at him. "I can manage on my own. Thank you, though." She turned and headed to the elevators next to the front desk.

"You sure you don't want any help?" Jack asked. She glanced back at him, and he gave her a wink, grinning smugly. "You might get that chance to try out that article of yours." He pointed at the bellboy behind the young man's back and wiggled his eyebrows.

Paige's mouth fell open. She snapped it shut and gave him a withering look. "Very funny." She punched the third-floor button inside the elevator. "That's *not* my article. Goodnight, Jackson."

"It's Jack!" he called out. But the elevator doors had already closed him out of view.

Her lips curved slightly with satisfaction.

The next morning at poolside, tropical flowers and jungle plants floated a fragrant welcome to Paige upon the warm, humid Hawaiian breeze. She had one hour to go before her ten o'clock group tour departed. A mountain hike along the Na Pali coast—her first chance for Operation: Experience Life and Live a Little, as Aunt Naomi had called it. Paige hoped to put what she'd recently read on the subject into practice.

She stepped onto the sun-splashed pool deck and admired the view. The resort lined three sides of the pool, creating an intimate enclosure that overlooked the beach, a mere stroll away. Vibrant sprays of red and yellow flowers cascaded their brilliance from rock planters. She liked how Club Lealea's balconies and patios were draped with island flora, creating a graceful botanical elegance.

Paige sighed. Unfortunately, there was nothing graceful, nor elegant, about the scene at the pool. Several diehard sun-worshippers were already at it. Dark, unhealthily tanned pectoral muscles slick with coconut oil…fake breasts on flagrant display…thong bikini bottoms, cheeks bared for all to see…and early-morning Bloody Marys sloshing about in the hands of lusty singles on recliners and at stools along the swim-up bar. Rock and hip-hop music blared from speakers, garishly punctuating the morning air.

Paige stepped over a pair of legs that blocked her path to an empty table. She tried hard not to look at the almost bare bottom that smiled up at her as she maneuvered over the top of its owner's legs. *Geesh. Why even wear a bikini top if you're going to leave it untied like that? Heaven forbid you get a tiny strap line across your back.*

How was she ever going to fit in at this place? She glanced at her conservative shirt and hiking shorts. Her outfit didn't exactly cry out "sexy, single and sizzlin'." She sank into a chair beneath the welcome shade of a patio umbrella. The smell of the pool's chlorine played heavily in the air.

She opened the backpack she'd prepared for the tour and double-checked its contents. Sunscreen, floppy hat for full sun protection, water bottle, binoculars, tour brochure, day planner, notepad, pen…what else? She shoved items to the side. Oh, yes, and there on the bottom lay her big color-photo botany book for identifying plant life along the trail. All set.

She glanced at her watch. She still had plenty of time before departure. She moved the ashtray to the other side of the table and gazed out across the deck, listening to laughter, splashes, and the occasional scrape of pool chairs against concrete. She noticed that the handful of Lealea employees, working poolside, all wore leis around their necks this morning. That was a nice touch.

Suddenly, Jack ambled into the area from the opposite end of the deck. Paige's breath caught in her throat. Annoyed at her reaction to the man, she frowned and covertly watched him from beneath the brim of her patio umbrella.

He looked cool and casual from the top of his sun-kissed, devil-may-care hair down to his khaki shorts. And he, too, wore a lei. He paused and calmly took in the scene. His eyes scanned the bar, the pool, and the guests as he strolled by the pool. He paused to shake a young man's hand and nodded to a group of women sunning themselves on reclining chairs.

He was certainly not the Jackson Banta Paige remembered.

Jack. It's Jack, she reminded herself. Of course, she secretly got a kick out of seeing him bristle when she used his full name. She watched him glad-hand a few more visitors and flash a grin at a redhead in a black bikini.

Yep. Definitely not the Jackson she once knew. In his element, strolling around the resort, the man was all Jack.

The awkward body and hesitant gait of the past had been replaced by a smooth step, graceful almost, his stride confident. Even the droopy palm trees seemed to bow respectfully to their handsome proprietor.

He leisurely searched the tables until he spotted her sitting beneath the umbrella. Their eyes met, and the bold throb of the hip-hop music danced in time with Paige's heartbeat. She watched him wend his way toward her.

Jackson Banta had turned into a playboy—managing, *owning,* a singles' club, of all things. And although he was the physical embodiment of her fantasies, he was far too…unsettling for her taste.

As he neared she noted how his features had grown more chiseled, more sculpted over time, and how his soft, youthful lips were firmer, more masculine.

Paige decided he'd probably dallied with all kinds of beautiful women at his resort. So even if she *was* interested—which she definitely was not, she reminded herself sternly—Jack Banta would never be attracted to a plain, socially awkward woman like her.

Jack made his way to Paige's table. He'd been hoping to find her before she left on her tour. He planned to spend as much time with her as possible during her stay at his club.

Who ever said paybacks were hell, anyway? By the looks of things, Jack would say paybacks seemed more and more like heaven.

He thought back to the plan he'd jotted offhandedly on a napkin last night after she'd checked in. A payback plan of sorts.

Making lists was an old habit of his, stemming from his nerdy days in school. And it served him well in business now, too. Yep, there was nothing quite like checking off items on his to-do lists. It made him feel productive, goal-oriented.

Number One on his plan was to show up at Paige's side, every chance he got—pay her attention, flirt a little. Basically get on her good side. Number Two would be asking her to dinner, a casual invitation, maybe a visit to his suite afterward, if things went well. Number Three, once she felt more comfortable with him, included a casual touch here and there, maybe sliding his arm around her, a caress if she was willing. And fourth, when the time was right, he'd move in for a kiss. Not just any kiss. But a kiss that would tell her what she'd missed out on all those years ago. A kiss to leave her breathless. *A kiss to remember.*

By her departure date, he'd have her kicking herself for ever thinking Jackson Banta wasn't good enough for her.

He grinned to himself and approached Paige's table, giving her his best charming, "Aloha!"

"Hi, there," she replied.

"Mind if I have a seat?"

"No, go ahead."

Check. He mentally checked off Number One. But he'd have to join her several more times before he could consider himself on her good side. He pulled out the chair next to her and took a seat. "So, did you get together with Lulu to book a spot for the hiking tour?"

She nodded, her black pony-tail bobbing against her shoulders. "It leaves at ten o'clock."

"Great." Jack liked the enthusiasm that made its way past her stiff exterior. Of course, she'd always been like that. Enthusiastic yet studious, always interested in everything around her.

She even looked the same as she had in school. He wouldn't say her face was striking, but he found beauty in its simplicity. Big dark green eyes, set against creamy smooth skin. A small, pert nose, just the right fit for her face. And delicate skin that rarely saw the light of day, if he knew Paige as he thought he did. Knowing her, she spent most of her time in the library. He smiled softly. Yep, that was Paige, all right.

"You'd probably like the bird-watching tour, too," he said.

"Bird-watching? When is it?"

"Next Wednesday."

"Really? How did I miss that?" She pulled the club's activities schedule out of her backpack and scanned the list of tours.

Jack studied her while she read the brochure. She'd always had a fresh-faced look. A look that brought to mind things like oatmeal cookies, Ivory soap…and chaste cotton panties. He swallowed.

"I don't see bird-watching on here, do you?" She held the schedule out to him and uncrossed her legs…her long, slender, bare legs…

Jack pulled his eyes away from the gentle slope of her calves and stared at the brochure she held out to him. What he would've given to have her by his side years ago. Just like this. The sun shining through her jet-black hair as she looked back at him expectantly. Except back then, he wouldn't have known what to do with her. But that was then…

"Don't you want it?" she asked.

Mother of God, yes. He shook his wandering thoughts from his head. "I'm sorry, what?"

She wiggled the pamphlet at him. "I said, I don't see bird-watching on here, do you?"

"Oh." He took the brochure and scanned it. "It's right here. Under 'expeditions'. The bus leaves Wednesday at one."

"Wednesday, hmm." She reached into her backpack again and pulled out her day planner.

Good Lord. How many things did she have in that pack?

She perused the planner. "I was thinking about trying the aerobics class that morning. And I wanted to catch the hula lessons right after that. Would that give me enough time to get ready for bird-watching? I'd hate to leave hula early." She chewed her lip and flipped to the next page. "But, if I take the afternoon hula class, I might have enough time for bird-watching, after all. Oh, but then there's the three o'clock yoga. I could try to go the following Wednesday—"

Jack reached over and took her day planner out of her hand. He shut it with a snap.

She blinked. "What did you do that for?"

"Are you kidding? My head was starting to hurt. You're on vacation. Why don't you live dangerously and have an unscheduled day? The tours don't fill up until the last minute, so why don't you play it by ear?" He grinned. "You know. As they say on the island…hang loose."

"Hang loose? Hmmph." She snorted primly and reached over, snatching her planner out of his grasp. She tucked it in her backpack. When she looked up, she frowned slowly and nodded to a spot over his shoulder. "Um, there's a chicken in the pool."

What?

Jack twisted in his chair.

Apparently, a free-range chicken had accidentally fallen into the water. Its squawk pierced the morning air, and the bird was flapping its wings like crazy, to no avail.

A guest, floating in an inner-tube, squealed and dropped her Bloody Mary in the water. "Eew, get away, get away!" She splashed back at the floundering chicken, and the chicken took that as an invitation to join her on her tube.

"That looks like hanging loose to me all right," Paige said.

"Aw, Jeez." Jack pushed his chair away from the table.

"Guess I don't have to schedule bird-watching, after all. Looks like I have a front-row seat right here."

Yeah, great. Jack noted her amusement and clenched his jaw. How the hell was he going to come off as suave and smooth while he chased a goddamn chicken out of the pool?

"Catch you later," he muttered. Reluctantly, he strode off to save the day.

Half an hour later, Paige sat on the tour bus alone, waiting for others to board. Just as at university, she was the first one to arrive. She sighed, watching out the window as singles gathered on the curb below.

Everyone at the club seemed to have already hooked up with someone, either as buddies or as couples. Three young women stood beside the bus, taking sips from their water bottles and fiddling with their backpacks. A group of guys stood off to the side, eyeing the women and talking among themselves.

Paige shifted in her seat, feeling very…alone.

Finally, two of the guys climbed the steps to the bus. The shuttle gently rocked with their weight as they came aboard. Both looked physically fit, one tall, the other stocky, muscular.

Her heart kicked up a notch as they ambled down the aisle toward her. She felt self-conscious all by herself. She wondered if they'd speak to her.

They made their way down the aisle, closer and closer, passing one empty row after another. She waited. Should she smile? Maybe say something? She knew she looked awkward, sitting there just staring at them.

Say something, her mind screamed. *Anything.* "Hi!" she blurted out.

Her voice seemed to startle the tall guy.

"Hey," he replied, giving her a polite nod. He continued past her. His buddy did the same.

Impressive, Paige. Nothing says "I'm fun and happenin'" like a monosyllabic "hi" blurted out full-volume.

The two guys took a seat a few rows behind her. Great. Now they were staring at the back of her head. And she was sitting there like a big loser.

Trying to act natural, she flipped through her tour brochure, silently willing the guys to speak to one another. To break this awkward silence. She slowly turned her head and glanced back at them. Yep. They were looking right at her. She gave a nerdy little wave. Heat slithered along the back of her neck, and she turned to face forward again. Mmm-hmm, good times.

In a few minutes, the bus mercifully began to fill. At first, there were only two people at a time, but later groups of three and four boarded. No singles, though, and no one taking the seat next to her.

Well, this was fun. Paige stared out the window as the bus grew louder with voices and laughter.

Soon, a handsome young guy climbed the bus steps and stood at the front, searching for a place to sit. When he spotted the seat next to Paige, he made eye contact with her.

She met his look and nodded slightly. Hmm, things were suddenly looking up. She pasted what she hoped was a pleasant, inviting smile on her face.

Cute Guy made his way down the aisle toward her, dodging feet and backpacks in his path. He pushed his hand through his dark wave of hair and grinned as he approached.

Suddenly, Jack appeared from out of nowhere behind him. He put his hand on the guy's shoulder.

Cute Guy paused and turned.

"Hey," Jack said. "How's it goin', buddy?" They shook hands.

What was Jack doing here? Paige watched the two men as they stood in the aisle beside her seat.

"Enjoying your stay?" Jack asked.

"Yeah, it's been great," Cute Guy answered. "You coming on this trip, too?"

Jack glanced down at Paige and grinned. "Yeah. I had some free time today and thought what the hell." He returned his gaze to the guy. "Listen, ah, Paige here's an old friend. Mind if I take this seat?"

Cute Guy shrugged. "No, sure, whatever—"

"Yo!" A group of young men a few rows behind them hollered to him and pointed at an empty seat.

The cute guy nodded at his friends. He looked back at her and shrugged. "Got some buddies back there. I'll sit with them. See ya later." With that, he continued down the aisle.

Paige watched him walk away. She'd just missed her chance to meet someone new, thanks to Jack.

Jack slid into the seat next to her. "A-a-ah." He eased back and stretched his legs out into the aisle. "Now, that's what I'm talking about. Nothing like some leg room for a good road trip."

Damn him and his sexy grin. And damn the masculine, outdoorsy scent that clung to his clothes. "Don't you have any waterlogged chickens to rescue?"

"All the chickens are present and accounted for." He yawned casually. "It's just one of the hazards of the job. Hope you were taking notes. But look who I'm talking to. Of course, you took notes."

"Seriously, why are you here?"

He shrugged. "I like to join our tours now and then. You know, to make sure they're running smoothly. Gotta make sure the guests are enjoying themselves." He reached into his backpack and pulled out a bag of cinnamon bears. He popped one into his mouth and nudged the bag toward her, a questioning tilt to his brow.

"No, thanks." She glanced away from his attractive features.

Lulu herded the last stragglers onto the bus and took a seat at the front.

The driver closed the doors, and soon the massive bus lurched away from the curb. In no time, they were navigating the island's winding curves.

Jack rested his arm casually over the back of her seat.

Paige's neck tingled where his arm touched her pony-tail, and the enticing floral scent of the lei he wore against his chest awakened her senses.

"It's your first big day on the island," he said. He looked around the bus and leaned closer to her. "See any hot prospects?"

Besides Cute Guy? Not really, unfortunately. "I haven't been looking," she fibbed. The bus took a sharp curve, causing her leg to sway into Jack's. She clenched her knees together, away from the provocative heat that emanated from her distracting companion.

"You know, I'm a little hurt," he said, munching on another cinnamon bear.

"What? Why?"

"Because you haven't asked me if *I'm* single."

She angled a look at him.

"Just so you know—" he wiggled his eyebrows "—I am. And to save you from asking your next question…the answer is yes. I *am* available."

Against her will, a chuckle escaped her.

He laughed along with her, his dark blond hair ruffling with the breeze that flowed through the half-open window.

She liked the sound of his laugh. It was easy, carefree and very…male.

"Just because I joined this club," she said, "it doesn't mean I plan to frolic around the island, you know…'on the make'."

He scrutinized her for a second. "I'm not sure I've ever seen you frolic, Paige."

"What?" She frowned. "I—I frolic."

He laughed. "Yeah, you're a regular rock star."

She snorted at the amusement on his face. "Believe me, Jackson. I've frolicked plenty."

"It's Jack." He looked her up and down. "And I'd still have to say I'm not convinced."

"That's just because I've never frolicked with *you*."

"Paige Pipkin. Is that an offer?" He glanced behind them. "I never pictured you as a back-of-the-bus kind of

girl, but I bet there's enough room back there to frolic—"
he lowered his voice to a bedroom level "—if you insist."

She rolled her eyes for his benefit. But she couldn't
help following his gaze toward the back of the bus.
Suddenly an image of the two of them sprawled out on
the big back seat came to mind—his blue eyes smoky
with desire, his masculine hands gliding along her bare
skin, hot and urgent…

She swallowed and glanced over at him.

Their eyes met…and held.

Just then, one of the passengers headed down the
aisle, jostling Jack's shoulder, pushing him closer to
Paige. Jack braced his hand against the window beside
her head.

His handsome face was close now. Close enough to
note the tempting trace of cinnamon that mingled with
his breath as he gazed back at her. His expression turned
quiet, steady, and seemed to mirror her own heightened
awareness. The engine noise and boisterous voices
receded into the background as Paige's attention
narrowed down to the vinyl bench seat she shared with
Jack, to the inch of space that hovered between their
lips. She drew in a shuddering breath and gulped.

Was he going to kiss her? He was near enough, and
suddenly she tingled with anticipation. *She wanted his
kiss.* She breathed in his scent—a pleasant, intoxicating
blend of cinnamon, sea breeze and earthy masculinity.
It was addicting. *He* was addicting. And in that moment
she knew if she leaned forward, just an inch, she could
close that space between their lips.

"Go for it, Jack!" A rowdy male voice rose up from the back of the bus, along with someone's wolf-whistle.

The crass whistle skittered along Paige's spine, reminding her where she was and jolting her back to reality. She cringed, and the connection between them shattered.

Jack pushed off from the window with graceful ease, back to his own side, as if nothing had happened.

Paige was left feeling weak and a little vulnerable from the thrill that had just rocked her world. She gathered her senses and straightened in her seat.

What was wrong with her, anyway? It wasn't like her to act like a sex-starved teenager. It must be the lascivious singles' environment, corrupting her thoughts.

Paige turned away from the alluring club owner and forced herself to focus on the scenery outside the window.

Who would have thought she'd ever have the hots for *Jackson Banta*?

CHAPTER THREE

AN HOUR later, beneath the canopy of the Kauai jungle, Paige stepped onto a black rock that jutted from the middle of a small stream. She held her arms out for balance and forded the water. Safely across, she let out a breath she hadn't known she'd been holding and glanced around.

Dense, tall trees rose from the marshy earth. Moss crept along the ground and slithered its way up tree bark only to trail back to the jungle floor in green fuzzy tendrils. She'd forgotten how beautiful the islands were. Especially Kauai, the Garden Isle.

Jack had hiked with her for the first half hour, until Lulu had pulled him away, asking him a question about the tour schedule.

Now, only the stream kept Paige company, chattering and gurgling over its rocks, while the warm, heavy air swirled thick—a ripe brew of humidity, foliage and mud.

Paige paused to study a fern beside the path and unzipped her backpack to pull out her plant guide. She glanced at the empty trail ahead of her. The rest of the group had already forged on without her.

She wished Lulu would spend more time pointing out the flora and fauna of the island. Wasn't that what a guided tour was all about? Didn't the participants want to learn something on the hike? She paused. Probably not. It was a singles' tour, after all. She supposed the goal was to meet other people rather than study botanical guides. Paige sighed. She knew she turned others off with her intellect and interests. She shoved the guide back into her bag and quickened her pace to catch up with the others.

Her hiking boots beat an earthy rhythm along the hard-packed red dirt path. Soon, the trail grew steep. She was out of breath by the time she crested the ridge.

At the top, the midday sun broke through the trees, beaming its smile through lightly dispersed clouds that formed a lei of welcome. Paige found the rest of her group, standing at a lookout point, viewing Na Pali's emerald tree-covered cliffs and the ridge-capped waves that pounded the shore below.

"Okay, everyone, listen up," Lulu said, raising her voice above the rest. "This is where we typically stop for lunch. You all should have your sack lunches that I passed out at the start of the tour. We'll take a half hour or so to eat. If you finish eating early and want to continue ahead, feel free. The trail ends one mile from here. And remember," she added, shading her eyes from the sun and glancing around at the group, "we carry everything out that we carried in. In other words, no trash left on the trail, okay?" She pushed her long black braid over her shoulder and waited for a collective murmur of agreement.

The hikers dispersed in small groups to claim their spots for lunch.

Paige was left standing with Lulu.

The friendly activities coordinator turned to her. "Enjoying the hike, so far?"

Paige nodded. She'd liked Lulu when they'd met that morning. "It was great. A perfect trail, with both dense jungle *and* ocean views."

"Good. I'm glad you liked it. The Na Pali coast is beautiful. Always a crowd-pleaser. Mind if I join you for lunch?"

"No. Please." Happy for the company, Paige motioned for her to share a large rock beside the trail.

Once seated, Lulu peered into her sack lunch.

Paige joined her and pulled her water bottle out of her backpack. She took a long, cool sip. At this elevation, the Hawaiian sun blazed as hot as a tiki torch. She glanced at the pretty native islander beside her.

"Have you lived here long?" Paige asked, using a question that her book, *Small Talk 101*, had touted as a perfect way to start any conversation.

"I lived most of my life on Maui. I just recently moved to Kauai when the new Lealea club opened here." Lulu unwrapped her sandwich. "How about you? Where are you from?"

"I've been going to school in California for several years. But, actually, I spent two years of high school on Kauai."

"Oh, really?" Lulu took a bite of her sandwich, her eyes fixing on Paige with interest. "Our club's owner went to Kauai High, too. In fact, I saw you sitting with him on the bus. Did you and Jack go to school together?"

"Same graduating class."

"Really?"

Paige nodded, taking a bite of her own sandwich. Ham, mustard and tomato on whole wheat. Not bad.

"So-o-o, did you come to Club Lealea to see Jack again?"

"Oh, no." Paige chuckled. "I didn't even know he owned the resort. It was a surprise to find him here."

"Oh."

Paige licked mustard off her thumb and looked up to find Lulu studying her intently.

"So," Lulu said. "What was Jack like in high school? Was he a jock?" She laughed. "I can totally picture him like that. Jack, Mr Big Man on Campus."

Hardly. Paige withheld a snicker. "I wouldn't have called him a jock, exactly."

Lulu nodded, as if she understood. "Okay. I'm betting he was a ladies' man, then?"

No-o-o. Not that, either.

Before Paige could come up with a polite description of Jack as a teen, Lulu interrupted. "Let me guess. You had a big crush on him. That would be typical for Jack. Did he ask you out?"

Paige nodded. "Yeah, but—"

"So, you dated?"

"Um, no. Not exactly."

Lulu looked confused.

"Is this rock taken?" An energetic male voice interrupted their conversation.

Paige glanced up to find Jack standing next to them.

Lulu smiled. "Have a seat! We were just talking about you."

"Oh, yeah?" He lowered himself onto a patch of grass and leaned his back against the rock. "No wonder my ears were burning."

Lulu reached over and tugged his ear. "That's because your ears are sunburned, silly. When are you going to start wearing a hat?" She reached into her bag and pulled out a bottle of sunscreen. She rose and bent over him, slathering a gob of the gooey stuff over his left ear.

"Hey," he said, leaning away. "I can do it." He took the lotion from her grasp.

She grabbed it right back. "I'll do it." She hovered over his other ear, but he swatted her away.

She relented but not before touching a dollop to the tip of his nose and laughing.

Paige watched the two of them, amused. They seemed to have a friendly working relationship.

But the more she watched Lulu, the more she started to wonder. Lulu seemed to touch him an awful lot. The same kind of touches Paige had witnessed Jack receiving from another woman at the start of the hike.

The woman in the group ahead of them had sent subtle smiles his way, eventually lagging back until she hiked side by side with him. And she'd kept touching his arm, too. Just as the activities coordinator was doing right now.

Lulu leaned over and asked Jack a question, her

fingers lightly resting on his forearm. Granted, it was a work-related question, but still—

"Hey, Lulu!" A group of singles standing at the lookout point called her, motioning for her to join them.

Lulu sighed. "Duty calls. I better see what they want." She rose and stuffed the remains of her lunch in her bag. "Talk to you guys later."

Paige watched her walk away, then turned to Jack.

He wiped the last of the lotion off the tip of his nose. "How did you like the hike?" he asked.

"It was great."

"Good. Glad you liked it." He reached into his bag and pulled out an apple followed by his sandwich. "What kind of cookie did you get in your lunch?"

She peeked into her bag. "Peanut butter, I think." She hated peanut butter. "How about you?"

"Chocolate chip."

"Mmm, my favorite."

"We can trade." He handed his cookie to her.

"Really?"

He nodded.

"Thanks." He'd been awfully kind to her since she'd arrived at his club—showing up at her side, making sure she was getting along okay. She was surprised he was spending so much time with her, especially with all the pretty women on this tour. She swallowed another bite of her sandwich. To fill the silence, she asked, "Have you always lived on Kauai?"

"No. I was born here, but I moved to California after high school," Jack replied.

"You did?"

"Yep. I went to UCLA on an academic scholarship and then took a job at a dot-com company. Bought low and sold high and got out at the right time."

She hadn't known that. In fact, when she thought about it, she realized she knew very little about his personal life. She studied the attractive man sitting next to her. "So, you went to college in California just like me."

"Sure did."

"And then you took all that money you earned and started Club Lealea?"

"Mmm-hmm," he murmured between bites. "Actually, I started a chain. I've got Lealea clubs on both Maui and the Big Island, too."

That *was* impressive. "You were a smart kid in school. I'm not surprised you did so well after college. But really, Jackson, singles' resorts? What is Lealea, anyway?" She enunciated the word out loud. "Lay-ah lay-ah. What does it mean?"

"It's Hawaiian. Most of the guests pronounce it wrong. The Hawaiians actually pronounce it Le'ale'a. It means…pleasure."

"Club *Pleasure*?" She made an indelicate snort through her nose. "Figures."

He bit into his apple, the crunch slicing through the humid air. "I like running my resorts," he said. "Nothing wrong with pleasure, having a little fun." He eased back against the rock and stretched his legs out, eyeing her. "I think we all could use a little more fun in our lives, a little drama. Even you."

"Drama? No, thanks. I prefer the quiet life rather than your so-called drama." She took a bite out of her own apple.

"Ah, I see. Is that why you tried out for the play in high school? You know, to avoid drama?"

A heated blush crept to her cheeks at the memory. She'd spent the first few months at Kauai High feeling socially isolated and shy, finding her only refuge among the other nerdy kids in the academic clubs. And she'd hated it. Deep down, she'd desperately yearned to fit in. So, going against her nature, she'd tried out for the school play simply because all the popular girls had been trying out for a part.

"So, you remember the play," she murmured, recalling how she'd hated herself for caring about her image back then.

"Sure do." He grinned. "Who knew that the quiet Paige Pipkin had a zest for performing in front of a crowd? An untapped ambition for the spotlight." He laughed, obviously finding the idea amusing. "Yep, that's Paige. Get her in front of a microphone, and you'll never shut her up. I'm surprised they didn't have to pull out the big hook and drag you off the stage."

She stared at the ground, nudging a pebble with the toe of her hiking boot. She'd always known that she hadn't fooled Jackson. She'd belonged on that stage about as much as the head cheerleader had belonged in the chess club.

"Well," she said primly, "colleges look for well-rounded applicants. I auditioned for the play simply to broaden my educational portfolio."

"I see."

She watched him take a drink from his water bottle, hiding a smirk. "Besides," she continued. "You auditioned for the play, too, if I recall." She remembered how Jackson had walked into the audition, quiet, unassuming and serious. Always so serious. Wearing his usual short-sleeved button-up shirt and old hand-me-down blue jeans.

He had scanned the room, calmly assessing the situation in his typical way, alert and controlled.

She'd known that he'd shown up for the audition simply because she was there. He'd had a crush on her.

She'd always felt his serious gaze during scholastic honor society meetings, in science class, just about every time she'd walked into a room. Yet she'd continued to reject him for a date. She'd been fighting demons of her own back then. Reserved and studious herself, aligning with Jackson Banta, the shyest, quietest boy in school would only have made things worse for her. Not that there had been anything wrong with him. He'd been a great study-buddy and friend.

Paige glanced at the man beside her now—no longer quiet and serious, but cocky, grinning and carefree. "You weren't exactly the life of the party yourself back then," she said. She watched him leisurely survey her crossed legs and move his eyes up to meet her pointed gaze.

"I was in it purely for the kissing."

Yes, she hadn't forgotten the kiss and, apparently, neither had he. To try out for the lead role, the finalists had had to practice the line that included a harmless peck on the lips. And to Paige's horror she'd been paired with Jackson.

He had recited the line, his face scarlet. Then he had taken a step toward her and slowly lowered his mouth to hers. His lips had trembled against hers, tentative and soft…and then it had been over.

Neither of them had won a part in the play. Paige remembered being annoyed by that fact, her annoyance compounded by having Jackson trail after her as she'd left the auditorium. She'd stopped and turned on him. "Jackson, leave me alone." She saw a flicker of hurt flash through his eyes, but he masked it immediately.

He stared at her silently, his gaze wise and assessing. Then he looped one arm through his backpack. "Don't worry, Paige. The next time I kiss you, it'll be because you want to, not because you have to." With that, he walked away.

She stared after him, and it was then that she realized there was a lot more to Jackson Banta than met the eye.

She met those eyes now, smiling back at her. They were adult eyes—charismatic, confident…alluring. But deep down lurked a keen intelligence, the only hint of the boy she remembered, veiled behind dark lashes and a carefree demeanor.

"I'm just surprised my boyish charm and dashing looks didn't win me the part," he said with a shrug.

A slow smile curved her mouth, and she shook her head. Boyish charm and dashing looks didn't exactly describe Jackson Banta back then. But she appreciated his bold self-analysis.

These days, the man had grown into that description.

He took a bite out of his cookie, and a single crumb clung enticingly to his bottom lip. She suddenly felt the urge to lean forward and lick that tiny crumb right off his full, sexy mouth. Paige glanced away from Jack and, instead, shifted on her rock. What was the deal with her libido lately? Nonplussed, she refocused her attention on the conversation at hand.

"If I'd won the part," Jack continued, "I would've gotten to kiss the head cheerleader who won the lead role. Now *that* would've been something. She was good-looking. Blonde, if I remember. Great body, too."

She saw him steal a peek at her.

"She was the whole reason I auditioned," he continued.

"Uh-huh." The corner of her mouth tugged upward. "And what was her name again?"

"Her name?" He scratched his head. "Yeah, right, her name. Of course I remember her name. It was Tina."

When he sneaked another look at her, she shook her head.

"Not Tina?"

"No."

"I know it started with a T."

"Tiffany," Paige said. "Her name was Tiffany."

"Oh, yeah. Tiffany." He lifted a shoulder. "I'll bet she was a great kisser, too. Probably way better than the girl I was paired with to kiss."

"Hey!"

"What?" He looked back at her, his face the picture of innocence. "Oh, wait a minute. Was that you I was paired with to kiss at the audition? Funny, I don't recall…" He tapped his chin as if deep in thought. "*Oh*, yeah. I remember now." He gave her a sorry look and shook his head. "I'm afraid your kissing wasn't all that good. You needed a bit more practice. But Trisha…now *she* would've been a good kisser."

"Tiffany. Her name was Tiffany."

"Oh, right. Tiffany."

CHAPTER FOUR

JACK remembered kissing Paige back in school, all right. How could he forget? He watched her tuck her empty lunch bag into her backpack.

He had to admit that he enjoyed spending time with her. Just as he had back in school.

He frowned slowly. Why *had* she turned him down all those years ago, anyway? Because of his looks? Granted, he hadn't been the captain of the football team…not by a long shot. But damn. Would it have killed her to go on a date or two? His mind wandered back to the hurt he'd felt, the rejection. It wasn't as if she hadn't known him well enough. They'd been friends.

The z-z-z-ip of her backpack awakened him from his thoughts. She tossed her water bottle into her pack and smiled at him. "Looks like the rest of the group has headed onward. We ought to catch up, don't you think?"

Hell, no. "Yeah, sure." He glanced around for a distraction that might keep them away from the others. "Hey, look at those flowers," he said, pointing to a clump of blooms beside the trail. "I wonder what those are called?"

She immediately took the bait and stooped beside him to examine the fragile white blossoms.

Yep, he knew Paige. She'd never pass up a chance to study something new.

Clearly forgetting all about the rest of the group, she peered at the flowers that peeked out from beneath an expansive fern. She was close to him now. Close enough to catch the faint whiff of hibiscus and sea salt that clung to her clothes and skin.

He was used to having women fall at his feet, these days. But Paige was different. Somehow he couldn't picture her ever losing her cool for a guy. The idea unnerved him.

Yet it challenged him at the same time.

He ran his eyes along her profile and over her hair, scooped into a pony-tail. Always scooped back, always untouchable. Yet one piece of hair had worked its way loose, resting along her cheek and curving with the line of her jaw.

She dragged her backpack near and took out her little black glasses, slipping them on. "Hmm. Nonfragrant. Shade-loving." She fingered the blooms and wrinkled her nose to adjust the glasses on her face.

God, she was cute.

He squatted beside her to take a closer look at the plant.

She pulled an enormous botany book out of her backpack and flipped through it.

Good Lord. Had she been lugging that thing around the entire time? No wonder she'd been bringing up the rear.

"Well," she said, taking off her glasses. "I'm not quite sure what this flower is." She squinted at the plant's leaves and rubbed one between her fingers. Then she inspected the underside. "It's got a bipinnate leaf form, so it's either one of these—" she showed him a photo of a similar-looking plant "—or one of these." She turned to another page.

Hell, he didn't care what kind of flower it was. It looked plain to him. White with a tinge of light pink. Nothing he'd call remarkable.

"Isn't it beautiful?" she asked softly next to his ear.

His neck tingled with her breathy question. Seen through her perspective, the flower wasn't so bad, after all, he decided.

She shifted her gaze to him.

He looked into her deep green eyes. "Yes," he said quietly. "It is beautiful." He ran his gaze over her pale, creamy face, her eyes a mist of moss-green and earthy brown shadows. He lowered his glance to her lips— tinged a subtle shade of pink, just like the flower. And close. Her lips were so close. He bet they'd feel petal-soft and sexy against his.

He swallowed and felt the nearness of the humid jungle all around them—the whir of insects, the tickle and scrape of leaves. He lifted his hand to her cheek and tucked the wayward piece of hair behind her ear.

"There you are!" Lulu broke through the philoden-drons that branched over the trail and tramped through the ferns toward them.

Reluctantly, Jack dropped his hand from Paige.

He shrugged off the nagging irritation that crept along his spine and sent a pleasant smile Lulu's way.

"Yes?" He and Paige rose and stood next to the flowers they'd been inspecting. "What's up?" he asked Lulu.

"Oh. Nothing. I just didn't see you guys at the trail summit and thought something must've happened to you."

Well, something might've happened if she hadn't come barging through the damned forest. Jack sighed. It was just as well. Going in for a kiss too soon might ruin his plan. He needed to take things slowly. Moving from Number One straight to Number Four on his list wasn't the way to go about it. There would be a better time and place for their kiss.

And when he did kiss her, he would savor every second of it.

As would she.

That evening, Paige ambled down the pathway past the club's pool, following the tiki torches that led to the luau. As she drew near muffled voices grew louder. She entered the area and glanced around.

Singles stood in small groups, talking and laughing, while others filled their plates with food at the outdoor buffet. Tables stood scattered across the sand, most already full with diners.

Paige swallowed and forced her feet forward. She hated mingling. She toyed with the lei that rested against her chest, the one Jack had given her the night before. She'd misted the flowers to keep them fresh. Lifting the lei, she inhaled its pretty scent.

She made her way through the crowd. So far, not a single face looked familiar. Perhaps she should sit at an empty table and wait for someone to join her. She paused. No, darn it. She'd come to this club to experience a few things, and sitting around wasn't the way to do it. She needed to introduce herself to others and make some friends.

Slowly, she wended past full tables, darting a shaky smile at strangers in her path. Her sandals sank into the gritty sand, tiny grains slipping beneath her heels and sneaking between her toes.

At the front, near the stage, a few tables stood empty. She found a lone man sitting at one.

He glanced around, looking very much by himself.

Her mind flashed back to one of the articles Aunt Naomi had slipped into her suitcase. "Ten Ways to Approach a Hottie and Leave With his Phone Number." Paige swallowed. Well, the guy would definitely fall into the "hottie" category. Not that she was after his phone number. But company for dinner would be nice.

A waiter paused on his way by, carrying a tray of cocktails. "Would you like a drink, ma'am?"

Sure, what the heck. Call it "the eleventh way to approach a hottie," she decided with a grin. She surveyed the selection of drinks—pineapple mai tais, strawberry margaritas equipped with tiny umbrellas, slender glasses of wine and frothy beers. She chose a simple white wine and thanked the waiter.

Stealing another glance at the hottie, she grimaced.

Time to dazzle. She took a sip from her wineglass and stepped toward the guy's table.

He turned his head her way.

Eek, he's looking at me. She paused, and her smile faltered.

Just then, a young woman with long reddish-blonde hair took a seat at a neighboring table.

Hmm. She looked nice. It seemed a lot less scary to approach the woman and ask if she could join her instead of approaching the hottie. Relieved at the new choice, Paige made a last-minute decision and veered toward the woman's table, instead.

Half an hour later, she relaxed back in her seat, glad she'd made the decision. Her new friend, Kathy, was an amiable young woman who'd arrived at Club Lealea the same day Paige had. After filling their plates with fine Hawaiian cuisine, they chatted together as they ate.

Kathy pushed her long strawberry-blonde hair over her shoulder and leaned toward Paige. "So, have you met anyone yet?" She put her hand to her mouth and whispered, "You know, met any cute guys?"

"Not really. You?"

"Not yet. But the trip's still young, isn't it?" Kathy raised her drink and clinked it to Paige's glass.

Paige laughed, liking her new friend. And she had to admit she was surprised by that fact. She'd assumed she wouldn't have much in common with the other vacationers at the meat-market resort. But Kathy had been nothing but nice, approachable…welcoming.

Paige took a cool sip of wine and stared down at the

delicate candles that floated in a crystal vase on the table, caressing the tabletop with soft light. Perhaps she'd been a little too quick to judge others at Lealea. She rolled that thought on her mind and glanced around.

A group of Hawaiian musicians climbed the steps to the stage, ukuleles in tow. It looked as if the luau was officially about to start.

One of the band members tapped the microphone and cleared his throat. "Ladies and gentlemen, we'd like to welcome you to the Lealea Luau. We're going to play some music for you. Please feel free to fill your plates at the buffet if you haven't done so yet. Afterward we'll have hula dancers on stage and a limbo contest. Stay tuned for that. *Mahalo*." He nodded to the crowd and picked up his ukulele. "Enjoy your meal." The band began to play softly in the background.

"Mind if I join you ladies?" a male voice asked behind them.

Paige and Kathy looked up to find a handsome man standing at their table, a plate of food balanced precariously in one hand, a beer in the other.

"Sure," Kathy said. "Have a seat."

He sat across from them and placed his napkin on his lap. "Wow. How did you two end up at this table alone? I'm surprised you haven't had to fight off the rest of the guys." He grinned.

"Well, maybe we *have* been fighting them off," Kathy responded. "And maybe you're just the first one we've decided to let sit here." She gave him a sassy grin.

He chuckled. "Guess tonight's my lucky night, then."

Kathy winked at Paige and answered, "Maybe it is."

Paige smiled at the flirty exchange. She wished she were as bold as Kathy was. She studied the handsome newcomer.

He seemed friendly. Accessible, interested. His dark shock of hair rested carelessly across his forehead, and his face was framed by a hint of stubble along his jaw.

"My name's Kurt," he said, taking a sip of beer. "Where are you two from?" His easy gaze flicked back and forth between them.

"I'm from California," Paige said.

"And I'm from Nevada," Kathy finished. "How about you?"

"Colorado. You guys come here together?"

"No," Kathy answered. "We just met."

"Ah."

"You look familiar. I think you were on the snorkeling trip I took yesterday," Kathy told him.

Kurt grinned. "Oh, yeah. That's right. I remember you. Red bikini, blue sun visor?" He chuckled and lowered his voice. "The one who got queasy on the boat-ride back to shore?"

"Oh, you noticed that?" A light shade of pink colored Kathy's cheeks. "That was a rough ride. The sea was cranky that day."

"Don't feel bad. It was getting to me, too." He gave her a good-natured wink. "I was just trying to play it cool."

Throughout the meal, Paige noticed that Kurt directed more of his attention to Kathy. They seemed to have a lot in common and were hitting it off well—the subtle glances, sending smiles to each other.

The band paused for a break, and four male dancers took to the stage, twirling flaming torches, their grass skirts rustling as they entertained the crowd to the beat of drums.

Once dinner plates had been cleared, the band returned to the stage, and soon Paige found herself alone.

Kurt had asked Kathy to dance, joining a group of couples on a makeshift dance floor along the sandy beach in front of the stage. Flickering tiki torches outlined the setting sun, and the twang of Hawaiian music played on.

Paige smiled softly as she watched Kurt and Kathy. She'd enjoyed their company and was pleased to make two new friends. She was happy they'd found each other. She supposed that was what singles' clubs were all about.

She rubbed her hands along her bare arms, warming them against the cool sea breeze that banked off the ocean's waves and drifted across the sandy outdoor arena. Shadowy palm trees dotted the pink horizon, and the muffled crash of distant waves filtered past the soft music.

Suddenly, a plate of key lime pie attached to a male hand and masculine forearm descended in front of her. Startled, she turned and looked up to find Jack grinning down at her, a cocktail in his other hand.

"Dessert for the lady?" he asked. "Your favorite. Key lime pie." He pulled up Kurt's empty chair and settled himself across from her.

A slow grin tugged at her mouth. Why did it feel so good to see him again? Annoyed by the feeling, she asked, "How did you know key lime's my favorite?"

"I remember a certain school Honor Society picnic where you went back for dessert...*three* times." He grinned. "For key lime pie."

That sounded about right. How did he remember that? She smiled sheepishly. "Thanks," she murmured. "It is my favorite." She cut a perfect triangle off the tip of the dessert. Mmm, sweet and tangy. She licked a dab of whipped topping off the side of her fork. The gentle breeze ruffled the white tablecloth, and she smiled at Jack, feeling rather spoiled.

Just then, Lulu took to the stage, lifting the microphone off its stand. She wore a coconut bikini top and grass skirt. "All right, ladies and gentlemen, is everyone having a good time? Let's hear it if you're enjoying your stay at Club Lealea."

The crowd clapped and whistled, and Lulu clapped along with them. "Good. Okay, then," she said. "We'll get back to the music in a little bit. But right now, it's time for a hula lesson for all of you who haven't taken the hula classes yet." She shaded her eyes and looked down at the sandy dance floor where couples had paused to listen to her. "I'm going to be looking for volunteers, so you guys get ready."

She turned to the band, and soon the musicians started in with hula music. Lulu swayed her hips in a sensual dance, her long, flowing hair cascading over her bare shoulders. She looked absolutely beautiful, and

Paige found herself mesmerized by the music and the sultry movements of the young woman's arms and hips.

Soon, Lulu danced down the stairs and tapped couples on the shoulder, asking them to join her on stage. In minutes, she approached Jack's side at the table and wreathed her arms around his neck. "You, too, handsome," she said. "Come show us how it's done."

Jack shook his head. "Oh, no. No way."

Lulu held up the microphone, her voice booming to the crowd. "What do you say, guys? Don't you want to see Lealea's owner up on stage?"

The crowd agreed with hoots and whistles.

Paige watched Jack reluctantly rise.

Lulu grabbed him by the hand and pulled him with her to join the others she'd invited on stage.

She taught the group how to move their hips. The show quickly turned comical as the less coordinated guys made awkward, jerky circles.

"Hula is about telling a story with your hands," Lulu said to the crowd. She took Jack by the waist and shimmied against him, her lower belly against his groin, a tempting little smile on her lips.

Paige smothered a snort and wondered exactly what kind of story Lulu's hands were telling Jack at the moment.

He played along, goofing off for the crowd, much to the onlookers' delight.

Paige shook her head. Such a change from the Jackson she'd once known. She narrowed her eyes as she watched Lulu touch Jack, and a nagging sense of irritation made a hula dance of its own down her spine.

What was that? Jealousy? She pursed her lips. She'd be a fool to feel jealous of Lulu. The woman was stunning. Paige didn't stand a chance against her. She shifted in her seat, frowning. What on earth was she thinking? Jack would never be interested in a woman like herself, anyway. And why would she even care? She wasn't after Jack in the first place, right? Now, more irritated at herself than with Lulu, she crossed her arms and leaned back in her seat.

Mercifully, the hula lesson ended, and Jack made his way back to the table. As he took a seat he rolled his eyes. "Yep. Nothing like getting up in front of a group and making an ass of yourself." He took a sip of his drink and shrugged. "All part of the job, though. Gotta keep the customers happy." The gentle winds took that moment to sift lightly through his sun-streaked hair. A few strands dipped onto his brow, making him look as if he'd just tumbled out of bed after a romp beneath the sheets.

God, he was attractive. Paige toyed with her fork and glanced down at the floating candles on the table. The fragrance from the yellow and white plumeria petals drifted along the water's surface.

"Would you like seconds on the pie?" Jack asked. "Maybe thirds?" He grinned.

She set her fork down. "Very funny. One was perfect."

He studied her through the candlelight, his gaze unhurried, casual. "You seem quiet. Anything on your mind?"

Other than fighting a ridiculous attraction to the man sitting across from me? "Nope. Nothing at all."

"Ah." He took a sip of his cocktail. "So, tell me about

Paige Pipkin. You know, I never really knew why you came to Kauai."

She raised her gaze to his and carefully folded her napkin. He'd never heard the story, because she'd never offered it to anybody.

"I heard something about you moving here," he said. "To live with your aunt?"

She cleared her throat. "My parents were ecologists whose primary interest was studying and photographing endangered species on the Skeleton Coast of Namibia."

"Really?"

She nodded. "My mother home-schooled me on the desert until I was fifteen. Then, they decided I ought to at least know what it was like to attend a regular school. So, they sent me to live with my aunt Naomi here on Kauai for my last two years."

"I didn't know that." He looked at her with interest.

"Mmm-hmm. I also spent every summer with Aunt Naomi since I was ten." She smiled softly, thinking of her aunt. "I so looked forward to those summer months. My aunt's the best."

"How so?"

"Oh, I don't know. She's just—" How did one describe Aunt Naomi? "She's just a lot of fun. And I can talk to her about anything. She used to talk to me about school, my classes…life. You know, aunt stuff."

He grinned. "Then you must've spent hours and hours talking about me, that dreamy guy in your class who was so smart and handsome. Tell her 'hi' for me the next time you speak to her."

Paige chuckled.

"So, what was it like, living on the desert?" he asked.

Hot and isolated. She lifted what was supposed to be an indifferent shoulder. "We went for months at a time without seeing another person. My parents were completely involved in their research." And, unfortunately, that meant they'd had little time to spend with their only child. The unwelcome feeling of rejection still stung, even years after the fact. Thank God for Aunt Naomi and her loving acceptance.

"Wow," Jack said, shaking his head. "What an adventure, living in Africa. Was it tough suddenly being dropped into civilization on Kauai? Well, if you can call this small island 'civilization'."

At his question, Paige let her gaze drift across the sandy beach toward the last hint of sunlight disappearing from the horizon. She'd been such a bookish girl, never knowing any other way of life. And being thrust into a high-school society had been a culture shock, to say the least. Not that she'd had much say in the matter at fifteen years old.

She smiled ruefully. "It was hard to fit in at the new school, that's for sure. I never felt like I really did…fully." *And things haven't changed much since then, have they?* She frowned at the unsettling thought.

"I think most teens feel like they don't fit in," Jack answered. "Even without living on the desert for years."

Paige recalled the Jackson of the past.

He was right. He hadn't fit in back then, either.

"Guess you got to know your parents well," he said. "Being around them all the time."

"You would think so."

But that hadn't been the case. Her parents had been even more studious and introverted than she was. Book smarts and intellect had been the only way she'd known how to communicate with them. Feelings and emotions were rarely expressed and never discussed within her family. She'd missed out on the typical teenage things—mother-daughter talks, shopping trips to the mall, making chocolate-chip cookies. She'd yearned to feel closer to her parents, but she'd been pushed to the side to make way for their research, instead. As a result, reaching out to others and forming bonds were foreign to Paige. And fear of rejection had kept her from trying…until Aunt Naomi had forced her on this trip.

Paige twisted her lips, deep in thought. A lot of things had been chosen for her in her life, when she really thought about it. Even this trip. She frowned, pondering the realization. She'd always been one to go with the flow, not making waves, just shrinking into the background and letting life happen.

Jack interrupted her musing. "And, now, you're following in your parents' footsteps, in a way," he said. "With your archaeology degree."

"I suppose that's true," she murmured. She glanced across the table at him. "I've always been interested in plants, animals, history. Living in Africa gave me an understanding of where humankind all started, genetically speaking. It's fascinating, really."

But what Jack had just said made her think. Had she

really been following in her parents' footsteps? Aunt Naomi seemed to think so.

Paige's parents were so reserved. So…unavailable. God, was she like that? She stared at the floating candles that twinkled from the center of the table. Yeah, she supposed she was. A gentle breeze separated one candle from the other two. After a moment, it floated back and bumped against its companions.

She raised her gaze to Jack. "My parents doled out their approval solely for academic excellence and intellectual pursuits. It didn't really foster a fun-loving environment to grow up in." She gave a half-hearted attempt at a grin to lighten her statement.

"Sometimes you can't always get what you want from your parents," Jack said. His eyes held a rare, serious edge.

"You sound as if you speak from experience."

"Maybe." He pushed his chair away from the table, and his face slid back into its typical easygoing expression. He nodded toward the stage. "They're starting the limbo contest."

She glanced toward the dancers, feeling a tad let down by his abrupt change of subject. She was starting to want to know Jack. The real Jack. Not the smile. But she sensed a hesitancy in him to share. She looked back at him, and he grinned, all traces of their conversation gone from his expression.

"Let me guess," he said. "You're not really into limbo contests, right?"

She wrinkled her nose. "No, not really."

"Good. Want to walk off the meal along the beach, instead?"

"Sure." She rose. That sounded perfect, actually.

He led her across the darkened sand, his hand at her waist.

Against her will, an annoying little thrill skittered along her flesh beneath his touch. She carefully tucked that thrill neatly back into place.

Soft path lights lined the club's walkway, leading to the ocean. Paige felt the chill of the salty trade winds that whispered along the shimmering moonlight. She smoothed back a strand of hair that had come loose in the breeze.

"I know close to nothing about the Banta family," she said, in another attempt to learn more about Jack. "Do your parents live on Kauai?" As they reached the water's edge she slipped her sandals off to walk more easily through the sand.

"My mother lives on the mainland now," Jack answered.

They ambled along the shore.

"Oh. Is your father still here?"

Jack ran his fingers through his hair, leaving a stray lock resting against his forehead. He remained silent for so long that she thought he hadn't heard her question. Finally he said quietly, "I was the result of an island fling." He glanced toward the waves that crashed into the beach. "My father never married my mother."

Paige was unsure what to say to this revelation. She waited for him to fill the silence.

When the silence forced him to continue, he elaborated. "My mother lived on Kauai and was vacationing on the Big Island of Hawaii when she met my father. When she got pregnant, he denied I was his, and she ended up returning to Kauai to raise me alone."

Through the muted light, Paige saw a tiny muscle flex along his jaw. "Do you ever see your father at all—you know, in your travels around the islands?"

"I've kept tabs on him."

"Do you ever plan to contact him?"

"He abandoned us. My mom tried to get child support, he refused and she dropped it. He made it clear early on that he wants nothing to do with her...or me."

"Oh, that's awful." She shook her head, thinking of the pain his father's actions must have caused. "So, is Banta your mother's maiden name?"

"No. She married a man named William Banta ten years after I was born. I took his last name. Then my mother gave birth to my half sister." Silence joined them for a few paces, accompanied only by the sound of waves and the soft shifting of sand beneath their feet. "William died in a car crash three years after he married my mom."

"Oh, my." Paige swallowed. "I'm sorry."

Jack nodded. "I'd just turned thirteen at the time, and he was the only father I'd ever known. He was a good dad for the short time we had him in our lives."

By then, they had reached a curve in the shoreline, and they turned back toward the club.

The smell of sea salt played heavily on the humid night air. Paige breathed in deeply. She never failed to feel fascinated by the contrast of the lush, humid environment of Hawaii compared to the stark desert of Africa where she'd grown up.

She hopped away from an errant wave that threatened to splash her bare feet. "So, it was pretty much just the three of you growing up? You, your mom and your sister?"

"Yep."

Shoulder to shoulder, they strolled along the beach. Water lapped at their darkened footprints in the saturated sand. Paige recalled Jack's quiet nature in high school, and suddenly she realized why Jackson Banta had been so serious.

He had endured a lot at a young age and must have carried adult responsibilities, trying to look after his mother and sister after his stepfather's death.

In that moment, it all made sense to her. She came to a standstill on the sand and grasped his forearm. "Is that why you own your singles' resorts? To shed the burdens of your past and live…you know—" she searched for the right word "—live wildly for a change?"

The corners of his mouth tugged upward. "Live wildly?"

She wasn't deterred by his low, easy chuckle. "You were such a smart, studious kid, Jackson. And now…" She raised her eyebrows and gave him a pointed look.

He rocked back on his heels with an amused smirk on his lips. "And now what? I'm wild? Women have called me a lot of things. I've heard intelligent, good-looking…" He grinned wickedly. "Even heard the best she's ever had a time or two. But wild?" He chuckled. "What makes you think I'm so wild?"

She scuffed at a small piece of driftwood with her toe. "You know. The drinking, the…the women, the parties, the bikini contests, the women—"

"You said women twice." A mischievous look slipped across his face, and he tilted his head. "Paige Pipkin. Are you trying to come on to me?"

"What?"

"Well, let's see. We've got the ocean, the moonlight, the warm breeze. And, now, you're talking about getting wild and mentioning women…" He lifted a shoulder. "If I didn't know better, I'd think you were trying to give me a hint. Maybe asking me to get a little wild—" he paused for a suggestive beat "—with *you*."

Her mouth fell open. *What?* Now, how did he come up with— She saw the teasing gleam in his eyes and shut her mouth into a firm little line. That was so typical of him. He was always taunting her. Always making light of things. Always— She let out a murmur of surprise when he reached for her waist and pulled her near.

"Maybe it's time you lived wildly, too," he said, his tone lazy and sensual. He was close now. Distractingly close. He studied her face, his keen eyes glittering through the moonlight, daring her. "I told you years ago, after school auditions, that the next time I kissed you it would be because you wanted me to."

He leisurely moved his gaze along her cheeks and over her nose, coming to rest on her mouth.

"Do you want to kiss me now, Paige?" he asked softly.

Her heart turned a crazy cartwheel in her chest, and she gasped. "Certainly not." She meant to look away, but instead she found herself staring back at him, mesmerized by the ready male awareness on his face. Her heart pounded in wild rhythm with the restless waves.

He released her to tuck a wayward piece of hair behind her ear. "You sure about that?"

Of course she was sure. He was the owner of the lewd resort. A man who strolled casually along his poolside where half-naked women threw themselves at him. He was wild…he was sexy…he was cocky…he was, she gulped, moving closer. Then he was lowering his head…and he was kissing her. Why wasn't she doing something? *Anything.* But she wasn't. She just stood there, holding her sandals in one hand and closing her eyes as he moved his lips gently over hers. And it had never felt more right.

CHAPTER FIVE

JACK savored the feel of Paige's lips beneath his kiss.

She tasted of longing, remembrance.

He'd meant to pull back after a quick kiss, but his lips lingered on her softness.

It was clear she thought he was a playboy. But she had him pegged all wrong. Granted, he allowed things to look that way. In fact, he found it rather amusing, truth be told.

Women responded to his playboy persona. A hell of a lot more than they had to the old one—*the Jackson Banta of the past*.

But Jack wasn't all that wild. Not as much as Paige believed, anyway. Sure, he'd had his share of women. But he'd used discretion.

He pressed his mouth more firmly to hers and changed the angle of the kiss. Her lips softened further in response.

Jack lost all train of thought and brought her fully into his embrace. He'd waited for this all his life. To have Paige in his arms, not turning away, not resisting his touch, but easing into his hands just like this. Pliant. Soft. Willing.

He'd figured he'd become a little jaded over the years. But being with Paige brought back memories, yearnings. Suddenly, Jack felt he was experiencing this kiss as if it were his very first time.

She kissed him back with an unpracticed charm, and his heart swelled. *Paige.* Her name echoed through his mind, along with uttered longings, words he'd never dare say out loud.

Reluctantly, he ended the kiss and took a step back, realizing he'd just rushed his plan. He hadn't meant to kiss her so soon. Oh, well. He'd have to make some minor adjustments to his list, that was all. Maybe one mind-blowing kiss wasn't enough. It sure as heck wasn't enough for him. And he wanted to leave her yearning for him, right? That *was* the idea.

Altering his list, he decided to go back to the wooing stage of the plan and then work his way toward another kiss. Nothing too heavy. Nothing resembling an actual "relationship". No messy emotions. No strings attached. No future arguments, break-ups, *rejections*—all the things that typically arose when commitment was involved. Just some well-orchestrated regret, on her side, when she realized what she'd once turned down.

Jack gazed at Paige. Her large eyes, usually analytical, stared back at him, unfocused, aroused.

Pleased, he decided she looked more beautiful than ever in that moment—the lines of inhibition momentarily gone from her face. Yep, he'd always figured there was fire beneath her uptight exterior. He hadn't meant to kiss her quite so soon, but he wasn't sorry it had happened.

And, technically, he could check off Number Two on his list—having dinner with her. *Check*. Although he'd only joined her for dessert.

Jack leaned forward to place one last kiss on Paige's mouth. It landed gently against the soft give of her lips. But when she leaned into that last kiss, he swallowed—hard. Self-restraint drained from him like the ebb of the waves against the shore. Damn, she was shooting his payback plan all to hell with the sexy way she molded herself against him. He deepened what was supposed to be the last kiss, while temptation danced, naughty and uncensored, through his veins. He found himself pressing the full span of his hand against her back.

"Mmm, Jack." Her arousing little sigh curled around him like seaweed, clinging to the rocky beach.

Jack. She'd said his name. Finally.

For the first time, he was no longer Jackson to her. Jack let the knowledge sink in, deciding that his name had never sounded so sweet.

Paige wasn't aware of dropping her sandals and curling her fingers into the front of Jack's shirt. All she was aware of was the feel of hard muscle beneath her palms and Jack's lips against her mouth. She hadn't been kissed in a very long time, and she couldn't remember it ever feeling like *this*.

Typically, her voice of intellect spoke up. But that voice sounded islands away as she whispered his name.

She'd never felt a hunger like this before, and the strength of it stirred needs she kept neatly covered at all times. The moment Jack had touched his lips to hers, rational thought had abandoned her, replaced by nothing but yearning. Normally she would analyze the oddity, but at the moment all she could focus on was the tickle of stubble against her cheek, the strong arms pulling her close, and Jack's hands, hot and urgent, sliding beneath the back of her blouse and gliding along her bare skin.

He smelled of sea breeze and tasted reckless, forbidden.

She closed her eyes and marveled at having an attractive man like him moving against her, warm, strong and wanting.

The thought echoed in her mind—*an attractive man like him.* Slowly, reality invaded the heady desire that cluttered her thoughts. What on earth was she doing? She felt Jack's heart beating as rapidly as her own as she untwined one finger after the other from the fabric of his shirt.

He was an attractive man, all right. An attractive *playboy* who owned singles' resorts and could have any woman he wanted. How many other women had he taken on walks along the beach? Just like this? Kissing, groping, relinquishing their bodies to him without hesitation? He probably collected lovers the way beachcombers collected seashells.

She stiffened in his arms. She was a fool.

Jack Banta was not her kind of man.

And at the moment, pressed up against him and allowing him to touch her, caress her, she wasn't any different than those women at the resort who threw themselves at him.

Well, he could keep his slick, coconut-oil hands to himself.

She pushed against his chest to end the kiss.

He released her immediately. Surprise mingled with concern on his face.

The quick release sent her stumbling backward, and she lost her balance, falling onto her backside in the sand. Just then, a wandering wave took it upon itself to straggle onto the beach and add insult to injury by soaking her shorts. She glanced up at Jack, and his concern switched to amusement.

"You should've told me about your love for the water," he said. "Is this another hint? That you'd like to go skinny-dipping?"

Her splutter sounded as if she were in immediate need of the Heimlich Maneuver. She wasn't about to go swimming in the nude, especially with someone like *him*.

He reached down and extended his hand to help her to her feet.

She allowed him to pull her up. Spying her long-forgotten sandals, she plucked them off the ground. Then she swiped wet sand off her backside.

"Need any help?" Jack's teasing grin resumed its usual spot on his vexing face.

Paige pursed her lips, the breeze caressing her heated cheeks, similar to Jack's earlier touch. She shivered. He'd touched her enough for one evening.

"I'm perfectly capable, thank you." She lifted her

chin with dignity. "I have some reading to do before bed. Goodnight." She turned toward the resort and marched off along the sand with as much elegance as one could muster in a pair of soaking wet shorts. Back to the comfort of her books.

"Sweet dreams," Jack called after her. His tone hinted that he figured he'd be in them.

The next morning, Paige sat in the sun on her third-floor balcony and scooted her room-service tray to the side. Nothing like eggs benedict and a sweet slice of cantaloupe to start the day. She wiped her mouth and tossed the napkin onto the now-empty tray.

She rose from her seat and gazed down at the bustling blue swimming pool below. Memories of the night before crept into her mind, sending sparkles across her spine—along the very spot where Jack's seductive fingers had dallied against her bare skin. His warm, large hands had felt thrilling, invasive…and she'd liked it.

Paige furrowed her brow. When was the last time she'd been touched like that? It had been a long, long time, that was for sure. And she'd never felt the thrill that she'd discovered beneath Jack's touch.

How could she have let that happen? She warded off a shiver of sensual excitement. Well, it wouldn't happen again. Chalk it up as temporary insanity. She'd been caught up in the moment with the moonlight, the beach, the waves… She leaned against the deck rail and forced her mind off of Jack, focusing instead on the scene below.

She really ought to be down there, among the others,

enjoying the pool, rather than hiding indoors, ordering room service. Wasn't that the whole reason for taking this vacation? Fighting her fears and attempting to socialize? Socialize with anyone *other* than Jack, she amended. She heaved a sigh and turned from the balcony to unpack her swimsuit.

Minutes later, she stared down at the swimwear she'd laid out on the bed. A full-piece with blue and white stripes, skirted with a white ruffle complete with tiny red anchors on the trim. Good Lord. *Ahoy, Matey!* She hadn't worn the thing since…well, she couldn't remember the last time she'd worn a swimsuit. She needed to "shake things up a bit", as Aunt Naomi had said, but going to the pool dressed like a nerdy sailor on shore-leave wasn't the way to go about it.

Paige chewed her lip. Did she dare buy a bikini? All the other women at the club wore them.

She sighed. She supposed she should. The resort sold swimwear in its gift shop. She could find one there.

She picked the full-piece up off the bed. Time for this swimsuit to walk the plank.

Paige dangled it from her forefinger and let it fall into the trashcan beside the bed.

Half an hour later, Paige strode along the pool, wearing her new bikini beneath her clothes, feeling rather pleased with herself. Her new suit was skimpy, but not too skimpy. She located an empty lounge chair and took a seat.

The warm Hawaiian sun streamed down from the clear blue sky, and lazy poolside noise punctuated the morning air—splashes, murmurs, the occasional plastic squeak of deckchair straps, creaking beneath the weight of sun worshippers.

Ah-h-h, this was the life. Paige wiggled her feet to dislodge the flip-flops from between her toes. Each sandal landed with a rubber slap against the patio. She tugged off her shorts and shirt and glanced around, suddenly feeling naked in the bright light of day. Her bikini top showed far more cleavage than she was used to. She glanced down at the pretty flowered bikini and swallowed. She actually looked—dared she say it?— kind of sexy. Maybe a little too sexy for her comfort level. She pulled out the sarong she'd purchased with her new suit and tore off the tags.

Paige rose and adjusted the wrap around her waist, liking the idea of a little extra cover-up. She tugged and twisted the fabric around her hips. What the heck? How was this thing supposed to work? She squinted down at the picture on the tag—a picture of a model, wearing the same sarong. Paige tied, then re-tied the garment. Annoyed, she frowned down at her hips. The fabric bunched and bulged at her waist. She didn't look anything like the model in the picture. She jerked at the bulbous knot she'd made. Great. Now it was stuck. Giving up, she left it as was and sank into her recliner.

The sun shone brightly, and she turned her face to the gentle breeze, deciding she ought to apply sunscreen. She reached into her bag and squeezed out a dollop of lotion, her mind shifting to her classes back home. It all seemed so far away—forgotten almost, fuzzy. The library, her studies, the classrooms… But she knew they were still there. Awaiting her return.

She shifted on her recliner and wondered what Aunt Naomi was doing. Probably holding all-night parties and playing the stereo full blast, since she didn't have Paige in the house, trying to study.

Paige smiled softly. She looked forward to her aunt's visit next week. Naomi had called and told her she'd found a flight to Hawaii. Her friend, Irene, was excited to see her, too. She'd offered Naomi a room at her house for as long as she'd like.

Paige stretched luxuriously on her lounge chair and grinned to herself. Yep, a girl could get used to this kind of life. Maybe this cheesy singles' club hadn't been such a bad idea, after all. Surprised by that thought, she raised her palm to her forehead and wondered if she was coming down with heatstroke.

After a few minutes of sunbathing, she grew bored. How did people lie in the sun like this, for hours on end? She slipped her reading glasses on and grabbed a copy of the morning newspaper off the table next to her. Turning to the first page, she noticed a handsome guy, watching her from a deckchair across the pool.

He smiled.

Oh, my. She smiled back, then glanced down at the breasts that spilled over the top of her suit. Amazing what a little cleavage could do for a girl.

She eased back in her lounge chair and perused the front page of the newspaper. When she lifted her gaze again, she found the guy still looking her way.

This time, he raised his glass to her.

Her eyes widened, and she gave him a hesitant wave. Was he nodding at her? Or someone else? She turned and craned her neck. Nope. No super models standing behind her.

Well…this is getting interesting.

She skimmed her eyes along the newspaper, not really reading, but trying to act casual. Maybe the guy would come over and introduce himself.

Suddenly, a rich, easy chuckle floated across the swimming-pool deck. Paige would recognize that low laughter anywhere. She glanced up to see Jack, standing behind the towel check-out counter, chatting with a female guest.

Easy male approval played across his face, and his reckless wave of blond hair looked as appealing as ever.

Hmmph. Paige raised her newspaper in front of her and snapped it into shape. So what? Jack was talking to some girl. Big deal. *Now, let's see what's in the news today…* She read the first column. GUBERNATORIAL ELECTIONS COMING SOON. *Fine.* TROUBLE IN THE MIDDLE EAST. *Typical.* HURRICANE HEADING FOR FLORIDA. *Not good.* She shifted her eyes restlessly down the page and heard a giggle.

Was it Jack and that girl?

She shook her head. Who cared?

Perspiration from the hot sun beaded along the bridge of her nose. Her glasses dipped lower. She pushed them up with her forefinger and peeked again at the handsome guy. Yep, he was still there. She smiled at him, then shifted her gaze to Jack.

He and his gal-pal looked fresh and cool beneath the shade of the towel hut. Their murmurs and chuckles drifted across the patio on the warm breeze.

Paige sighed. Jack could flirt with anyone he wanted to. Besides, she had a handsome guy watching her from across the pool. She turned the page. Hmm, BEST KEPT SECRETS TO SAVING ON YOUR TAXES…*interesting*.

Another titter of laughter echoed from the towel counter. She rustled the page and continued reading. Kittens for sale, purebred Siamese. Armoire for sale, cherrywood veneer. What? Wrong section. Now, where was the tax story she'd been reading? She pursed her lips, annoyed that she'd been distracted by Jack.

If anyone was going to distract her, it ought to be Handsome Boy from across the pool. She gazed over at him and nodded when he grinned.

She flipped to another page. *Here we go.* ECONOMIC OUTLOOK FOR THE NEXT YEAR. She read two lines and paused, peering over the top of the paper.

Jack and the girl were still at it. Why didn't Miss Laughs-A-Lot just check out a damn towel and get it over with? By the looks of things, the young woman was the one doing the checking out. Checking out Jack.

Paige snorted and raised the newspaper again. *Okay…news…news… What's going on in the world today…?* She flipped to the financial section. After a moment of scanning, curiosity got the best of her, and she found herself sneaking a look at Jack once again. The young woman had just left his counter.

Now alone at the towel hut, he glanced over at Paige.

Embarrassed by the way she'd clung to him on the beach the night before, she quickly snapped her paper in front of her face. Feeling Jack's eyes on her, she wondered if he was remembering the same thing—his soft lips moving against hers, his warm hands slipping beneath her blouse…

She coughed, more like choked, and tried to look casual reading the paper, as if she didn't care what he thought. What about her new bikini? Did he like it? Did she fit in with the other women at the pool?

Was he still looking at her?

A moist sheen formed at the nape of her neck. She felt hot and self-conscious, and her bare legs had started sticking to the lounge chair. Adding to her discomfort, her sarong had bunched up around her waist for the third time.

Unable to stand it any longer, Paige gave up the pretense of looking cool and casual. She smacked the newspaper on the table beside her and stood to untangle the knot in her sarong. She pulled the wrap from around her hips and spread it out in front of her. Should she fold it in half like this? No, that looked all wrong. Maybe making a triangle would work. Nope. She re-folded the wrap and frowned at it.

Suddenly, masculine arms snaked around her waist from the back. "Here, let me help." In two seconds flat, her sarong was tied in a tidy knot off to the side, the fabric smoothly hugging her hips.

She gasped and turned.

Jack stood grinning down at her. He shrugged.

"Someone had to do it. I've never seen anyone have so much trouble."

Paige glanced down at the bright floral fabric. The wrap molded to her hips, clinging along her legs and ending in dainty tassels above her ankles. Just like the picture.

She sniffed. *Figures.* He probably knew how to put one on so well from all the practice he'd had taking them off.

"So, I take it you're not going for a swim this morning?" he said.

"Why do you say that?"

"You never checked out a towel."

"Oh. Were you at the towel station? I hadn't noticed," she lied.

"No wonder. You've had your nose buried in the newspaper."

She reclaimed her seat, and Jack took the recliner next to hers, stretching out his legs.

Paige flicked a glance at Handsome Boy. He was watching her talk to Jack, the flirty smile now gone from his face. Damn.

Why was Jack sitting with *her?* Surely there were other guests to distribute towels to.

She looked at the sexy club owner by her side. He was close to her now. The picture of confidence, all wrapped up with a bold sexuality that simmered just below the surface.

Tanned and relaxed, Jack fit in well at his resort.

And she couldn't help but notice his perfect form. Soft, stroke-me skin, pulled taut across hard biceps that rippled when he moved. Paige swallowed and found herself pondering again how long it had been since she'd been, er, intimate with a man. The feel of masculine hands all over her. Encircled by strong arms, his body melded to hers in a hot, rhythmic straining toward release. Sensual words of pleasure uttered from a lover's lips…

She stared at Jack's mouth with a wistful sigh. Who was she kidding? Had she *ever* had hot, steamy sex like that? No. Not that she could recall…

Jack leaned over with a tempting gleam in his eyes and gently brushed his thumb over her parted lips.

"Mmm," she moaned softly.

Paige gave a start in her chair—jolted back to the moment.

Jack hadn't leaned toward her. He hadn't touched her lips. She'd just imagined it. Appalled by the throaty sound she'd just made, she sat up straight and cleared her throat.

"You okay?" he asked, gazing at her from his recliner with a curious look.

"Uh, yeah. Sure. The, um, heat must be getting to me." *His* heat. She fanned her face with the newspaper and then opened it. Adopting a nonchalant expression, she perused the first page she turned to. She felt Jack watching her.

"See anything interesting?" he asked.

"I always find the happenings of the world interesting," she replied with an aloof air she didn't feel. She angled a glance at him over the top of her glasses. "It's wise to stay informed." She scanned the page, not really seeing it. Could she feel more foolish than she did right now, sitting there ill at ease in her body-baring bikini? Nothing but a mass of perspiration and self-consciousness. Not to mention her lust-filled imagination that had a mind of its own. "Mmm-hmm. Good to be informed," she repeated, turning the page casually.

"Informed, hmm?" Jack leaned over and looked at her paper. "'Single white male, seeking huggable, sun-loving Capricorn to travel the islands.'" He arched a brow. "Ah, yes. One can never be too informed about the goings-on of the personal ads."

What? She glanced at the page she'd turned to. *Great.*

"No, wait a minute. Here's one." He leaned closer and read out loud, "'Mullet-wearing country-music teddy bear looking for single woman who loves to boot-scoot and talk dirty.'" He glanced at her feet. "Ever wear cowboy boots?"

She gave him a withering look.

Ding! The bell at the towel hut rang out across the patio. A young couple waited for assistance at the counter.

Jack rose from his chair. "The towel guy called in sick at the last minute, so I'm filling in." He stretched casually, his shirt rising above the waistband of his low-slung shorts, exposing an inch of hard, muscled abs.

Her mouth went dry.

"You look good, by the way," he said. His sensual gaze glinted with admiration. "Nice bikini."

Blushing hard enough to break capillaries, Paige shrugged, feigning indifference. "Just something I threw on."

"Listen," he said before leaving. "We've got a phone

at the towel hut if you want to call one of those guys you circled in the personal ads."

"What? I didn't circle anyone."

"You didn't? Think about it. They sell cowboy boots in the store just down the street." He chuckled and headed back across the pool deck, this time doing a goofy cowboy shuffle for her benefit.

Before she knew it, a bubble of laughter broke free from her throat. She glanced at Handsome Boy.

A buxom blonde in a white bikini had joined him.

Paige's smile slowly faded. *Damn it, Jack.*

How was she supposed to meet someone when he kept popping up at her side like that? She sighed and reached for the paper once more.

CHAPTER SIX

ON HER second week at the resort, Paige entered the cool, air-conditioned exercise room at the club, rather excited about her first workout at the gym, finally brave enough to step more fully into the singles' scene. The excitement in her chest expanded when she saw Jack chatting with a group of singles, waiting for the class to begin. She hadn't known he'd be taking this class today.

Over the past week, she'd grown accustomed to Jack's attention—his inquiries into how she was getting along, his checking-in to ask if her accommodations were to her liking. It made her feel taken care of, and, in a way, more secure. And she did appreciate it, she just wished he had a better sense of timing. Nine times out of ten, he'd interrupted her conversation with an attractive guest whom she'd just gotten to know, or filled the seat next to her at the club's Movie Night before anyone else. She smiled to herself and shook her head. Oh, well. He surely hadn't done it on purpose.

She crossed the gym and grabbed an aerobic step. She'd never taken an exercise class before, but how hard could it be? Just do what everyone else did, right? Heck, she'd made it through her classes at Stanford, so a simple gym class ought to be a cakewalk in comparison.

She set the step down and went back for dumb-bells, glancing at the surroundings. Wow, spandex everywhere she looked. Breasts overflowing tight sports bras, stretchy material pulled taut across muscled buttocks. Paige looked down at her own outfit. Baggy shorts and a tee shirt. She expelled a breath. Well, she didn't have to squeeze herself into some slinky get-up just to get in a good workout, did she? Surely, what she was wearing would do just fine.

From her spot near the back of the room, she found her gaze drifting toward Jack's corner. He was talking with two girls and a guy. He must've said something funny, because the group laughed. As he raked his fingers through his dark blond hair his eyes snagged Paige's gaze in the mirrored walls of the gym. Recognition registered on his face, and he turned to her with a wave.

Her heart lurched, and she waved back.

He looked good. *Too good.*

Judging by his physique, Jack obviously worked out on a regular basis.

Paige glanced around the room and swallowed a sudden rush of uneasiness, wondering if this was such a good idea. She typically maintained a decent shape, physically speaking, but maybe a step-aerobics and weight-training program was a tad ambitious for her very first class. She'd thought it sounded like a good way to try something new—try something *social*. But surveying the sleek, half-nude, muscle-bound participants in the class, she suddenly questioned her own physical ability.

Just then, Lulu entered the room, looking fit and trim in a tight aerobics outfit. She wore a microphone headset and took charge of the group as soon as she entered.

"Good afternoon," she boomed out in an enthusiastic voice above the murmurs and scuffling. "Welcome to the Monday afternoon exercise class. Our instructor can't be here today, so I'm filling in. It's nice to see all of you." She beamed her lovely smile at the crowd. "Let's start by forming three lines, facing the front, okay? And be sure to give yourself plenty of room." She waited while the singles shuffled into place. "Perfect." She clapped her hands together. "Let's have a great workout!" She turned on some jazzy music that exploded through the speakers in the walls. She adjusted the volume and took her place at the front. "Okay, everyone. Own your space, and let's do some deep breathing and warm up."

Paige lingered in the back row, while Jack took a spot in the front line. She noticed he was standing next to Kurt, the man she'd met with her friend Kathy a week ago at the luau.

Oh, and there was Kathy. Right next to Kurt. They must've gotten together. Paige's eyes met with Kathy's in the front mirror, and Kathy turned and waved excitedly to her. Paige grinned. All right. Maybe this was going to be kind of fun, after all.

An upbeat tempo blared through the speakers, and it appeared that everyone in the class had attended this workout before and knew what to do.

Paige mimicked Lulu's moves the best she could, spreading her feet shoulder-width apart and breathing deeply as instructed.

She took a deep breath in. Okay, this wasn't so bad. She let her breath out in a gentle whoosh. Then breathed in again. *Breathing. No biggie. She did it every day. This was easy.*

"All right," Lulu said through her headset. "Now march in place."

The group stepped briskly, and Paige glanced at her image in the full-length mirror. She looked silly, stepping in place like that. Oh, now wider marching? Paige spread her knees farther apart and imitated Lulu at the head of the class. Wide, awkward steps. Paige felt ridiculous. And her shorts weren't helping matters. Baggy as they were, they still constricted her movement— there was no give to the fabric. Suddenly stretchy spandex didn't sound like such a bad idea.

Paige glanced at Jack. Not bad. The view of his backside from where she stood was perfect. Blue shorts and a tight gray tee shirt stretched across a muscular frame—smooth, strong and sexy. He even made this ridiculous marching look good. The man was definitely coordinated.

Paige studied her own gawky moves and groaned. Suddenly, she realized that Jack was watching her. In the mirror. Their eyes met, and he grinned.

Oh, no. So much for hiding in the back of the room, going unnoticed. Great.

Lulu's voice called out above the music, cheerful and motivating. "Okay, guys, let's kick things up a notch."

In no time, Paige was puffing and sweating as she tried desperately to follow the group's moves. Step, clap, turn, twist, what? The rest of the class followed in perfect synchronicity, but Paige floundered. She went left when the class went right. She bumped into the unfortunate woman next to her and apologized, only to lose track of the next move altogether. She thought she saw Jack chuckling at one point, but she wasn't sure.

Paige fumbled her way through, counting the minutes until her humiliation would be over. Was that a blister forming on her heel? She sighed.

Near the end of class, she'd worked up a sheen of perspiration that matted her pony-tail to the back of her neck.

Who'd have thought that a simple exercise class would be so hard?

"Nice job, everyone," Lulu said cheerfully. She looked as fresh as if she'd just had an afternoon nap in the shade.

Did the woman always look perfect?

Paige swiped the sweat from her brow and glanced Jack's way for the umpteenth time, liking how his cotton shirt molded to his broad shoulders. He looked completely unruffled by the grueling workout. His dark blue shorts clung to his firm rear end, and Paige couldn't help but notice the muscular flex of his backside with every move. The rhythmic exercises brought to mind a raw, earthy image of Jack engaging in "other moves" that he'd probably be very good at. *Very* good, indeed. She swallowed.

Kurt, next to Jack, had taken his shirt off during the workout. Paige appreciated his nice form, too. But she liked the fact that Jack had kept his shirt on. It seemed less…blatant. As if he knew he had a nice body and didn't feel the urge to show it off.

"Time for squats," Lulu said above the music. "Grab your dumb-bells."

Squats? Even the word sounded uncomfortable. Exhausted, Paige sighed and picked up her dumb-bells, not sure how much longer she could last. Reluctantly, she followed Lulu's instruction.

"Squat down with your weights at your side like this," Lulu said to the group. "And hold it. Good. Slowly stand back up. Now, down again, hold it, feel the burn, and up. And down, hold it—"

Ri-ip!

Paige's shorts ripped in the middle of her squat. *Eek!* She reached behind her to feel how big the tear was. Yep. It was big. At least big enough for her underwear to show through. Her *granny-panty* underwear. Damn it all. She supposed she really ought to buy some decent-looking undies. For unexpected times like these. It was just that granny-panties were so comfortable. And, frankly, she hadn't planned on flashing the entire gym class today.

She sighed. Well, it should make for an interesting walk back to her room. She realized that no one had noticed her rip over the din of the music and their own exercises. Thankfully, there was no mirror behind her. If she kept her backside to the back of the room, all would be fine.

"Okay," Lulu said. "Let's get our heart-rates up one more time before we finish. How about some lunges, with our dumb-bells, to the beat of the music?" She lunged down, then up, down, then up. The class followed suit.

Paige lunged awkwardly. "Oof." This wasn't easy. And, yes, she definitely felt a blister on her heel now. Damn.

"Okay, now to the left," Lulu called. The class faced the left. "Down, then up. Down, then up. Okay, now, to the right."

Paige huffed out a breath and lunged to the right. Lord. How much longer was this class going to last?

"Now face the back of the room," Lulu said. "And lunge…"

Paige froze.

The entire room turned to her.

Uh-uh. There was no way she was turning her rear-end toward the entire class. The group lunged in synchronicity, and she just stood there.

Jack frowned in question at her.

She gave him a feeble smile and shrugged. Then she did the only thing she could think of…she knelt down and pretended to tie her shoe. That was it, she decided. She was *so* buying cuter underwear right after class.

Within minutes, Lulu concluded the workout.

Paige let loose a sigh of relief. Disaster avoided…so far. Hobbling from her blister, she edged her way around the room, putting her weights and step away. Now if she could just sneak out of there unnoticed—

"Paige!"

Her friend Kathy stood next to Jack and Kurt, beckoning her to join them.

Paige's heart sank. She waved back reluctantly and carefully made her way over. Cool air wafted through the hole in her shorts. She grimaced.

"Hey," Kathy said in greeting as she neared.

Paige clasped her hands behind her, covering the rip and trying to look natural…or breezy, as the case might be. "Hi, there," she replied.

Kathy smoothed her long, strawberry-blonde hair away from her damp brow. "It's good to see you again."

"You, too." Paige positioned her rear-end to the back of the room without mirrors. She glanced at Jack.

He smiled. "Great workout, huh?"

Heck no. "Yeah. It was fantastic." She twisted her upper body and stretched, trying to look like a workout pro. She swallowed a murmur of pain.

Kathy slipped her arm around Kurt's waist. "We're off to ride horses at Kokee State Park. Want to come?"

After the workout she'd just suffered? Sure. A bone-jarring horse ride ought to be just the thing to make her afternoon complete. "Um, no, thanks." She tried to look disappointed. "I already have another commitment. Maybe next time."

Kurt nodded. "Okay, then. We've gotta run. It's good to see you."

Kurt and Kathy said their goodbyes, and Paige

watched the couple exit hand in hand. A twinge of longing tugged at her as she watched them leave. They'd found what they were looking for. She cleared her throat and turned to Jack. "Looks like Club Lealea's made a love connection."

His lips curved to a half smile. "Yep. That's what it's all about." He grabbed his discarded gym towel off the floor and collected his things.

Paige took the moment to study him. The easy laugh lines around his eyes made him appear youthful, carefree on the surface. But, lately, she'd sensed a hint of depth to his personality. Something more complex lurking beneath his playboy demeanor. In fact, she was sure of it. After all, a person couldn't change all that much, and she once again found herself wondering about the man beneath the smile. Surely, there was more to Jack than raw sex appeal and fun and games.

What about the Jackson she used to know? The kind-hearted guy from school who'd worn his emotions on his sleeve? The guy who'd saved her a seat in the school cafeteria, the one who'd listened to her with that wise, intent spark in his gaze, the responsible student with whom she'd competed for valedictorian and practiced debate speeches with until they'd dissolved into belly laughs, too exhausted to think straight?

She looked back at the charming blue eyes that grinned down at her now and tilted her head, scrutinizing him. Jackson was in there somewhere, wasn't he?

All wrapped up in a hot, new package? A lethal combination, really, when she thought about it.

"Listen, I've got to get back to work," he said, running a careless hand through his hair, leaving it in a sexy jumble. "But aren't you signed up for the bird-watching tour this Wednesday?"

She nodded.

"I'm off that day, so I thought I'd join the tour, too," he said. "I have a great book at my place that has color photos of the birds of Kauai. If you'd like to come over tonight, we could check it out, maybe have a drink or two."

She raised her eyebrows. She'd love to study up on the birds before the trip. But it sounded suspiciously like…a date.

Just then, Lulu walked up. "Hey, guys. You two are in your own little world over here—the only ones left."

Paige glanced at the empty gym and realized she was right.

Lulu squeezed Jack's biceps. "I must've done a good job today," she purred. "'Cause you're looking stronger than ever." She smiled up at him.

Paige's heart dropped.

"Thanks again for filling in," Jack replied. "You did a nice job."

Lulu nodded and shifted her gaze to Paige. Her eyes cooled a bit. "Enjoy the workout, Paige?"

Paige nodded too many times. "Yep, yep. Great workout. Just what I needed."

"Well, you did all right for your first time, I suppose."

For her first time, huh? Gee, was it that obvious?

Paige twisted her mouth, the gaping hole in her shorts taunting her.

Jack frowned. "Your first time? Don't you exercise at home? You seem in good shape to me."

Pleased by his compliment, she smiled sheepishly. "Well, uh, I don't really work out often, *per se*. I keep in shape mostly—" heat crept up her neck "—mostly from running to and from classes at the university." She squeaked out a laugh and shrugged. "You know, going up and down the stairs at the library, carrying my books, my heavy backpack…" *Lordy, just stop talking.* How much more of a geek could she come across as?

She saw a superior expression glide across Lulu's pretty face. Yep, Lulu had just sized her up and found her lacking.

Humiliation danced through Paige's chest.

She turned to Jack. "Well, I've got to run. I know you have to get back to work." She slid a glance at Lulu and added for her sake, "And about tonight, Jack? I'd love to come over for drinks. Thanks for the invitation."

Lulu's face fell.

Paige felt the surge of victory. "See you at eight?"

"Yeah, sure." Jack nodded. "Eight it is."

Paige gave him a super-sized smile for Lulu's benefit. "Great. It's a date, then."

Paige glanced at the doorway. It was a good fifteen feet away. She nodded at them awkwardly and started backing toward the door, still facing them.

They watched her.

She grinned. "Yep. See you later." She kept backing

out, smiling and nodding, her hands clasped over the rip in her shorts.

Jack cocked his head, questioningly, clearly baffled by her ludicrous exit.

Once Paige turned the corner out of sight, she sagged with embarrassment. God, she must've looked like a fool.

And what had she said? That it was a *date?* Where had *that* come from? What if Jack hadn't meant for it to be a date, and she'd just turned it into one—with her giant smile and her suggestive tone? Then again, what if Jack *had* meant it as a date? Either way, it wasn't good.

What a day. It hadn't turned out anywhere close to what she'd planned. She nudged the shoe off her blistered foot and hobbled for her room. *Ow...ow...ow...*

Yep, good times.

So, they had a date, huh? Jack watched Paige back her way out of the gym. He wasn't sure why she was walking like that, but he didn't care. All he cared about was that they had a date. *Check.* Item Number Two of his payback plan, fully complete. Pleased, he congratulated himself on his idea to buy the bird book the day before. Heck, he didn't know all that much about birds, but he liked that Paige did. He appreciated her interest in the world around her, and it had given him something to do with her, share with her. Just what he'd hoped for.

A tug of anticipation traipsed through his gut. He'd

thought she would turn him down if it sounded too much like a date, but, hey, she was the one who'd said it. He watched her leave, a soft smile playing across his lips, until she was out of sight.

God, she was cute.

"God, she's a geek."

Pulled from his reverie, Jack frowned at Lulu next to him. "What did you say?"

The club's coordinator seemed to catch herself. "I mean, uh, you know. She's a total bookworm, don't you think?"

He grinned. Yeah, that was Paige, all right. And he thought it was cute. "She's smart, that's all."

Lulu shrugged. "If you like that sort of thing."

Come to think of it, he did. He'd always been impressed by her keen intellect. That was exactly what he liked about Paige.

"So, you're having drinks with her tonight?" Lulu's eyes narrowed slightly. "What's between you two, anyway? Were you guys an item back in school?"

Jack glanced down at the gym floor. No, no, they weren't. But that had been Paige's choice, not his. He remembered the disappointment, the unanswered longing, as if it were yesterday. The reminder drew his lips into a firm line. "Nope. We didn't date." He carefully schooled his expression to indifference. "Listen, I've got to get back to work. Shall we?" He gestured toward the entry, but Lulu stayed rooted to the spot.

She tilted her head, studying him. "Paige told me the same thing. That you two didn't date."

"Oh, yeah?" His skin prickled, and he paused. "What else did she say?"

Lulu toyed with her long black braid. "She said you asked her on a date, but you two never ended up going out." She angled a look at him. "Why is that?"

He shrugged. He wasn't about to discuss his personal life with his activities coordinator. It was none of her business.

Lulu continued. "I can't imagine why she'd turn down a guy like you." Then she added suggestively, "I wouldn't have."

Her last words echoed in the silence of the gym.

Oh, yeah? Well, he looked a little different these days than he had back in school. He wondered if her words would've been the same back then. Besides, he'd made it clear when he'd hired Lulu that he frowned on employee fraternization. It wasn't appropriate, especially not when he was her boss.

"Yeah, well." He lifted a shoulder. Paige may have turned him down back then, but he planned to make up for it tonight. At his place. With a few drinks and candlelight. A slow grin tugged at the corner of his mouth. He grabbed his towel and headed for the door. "Do me a favor and lock up the gym, will you?"

"So, let me get this straight," Lulu said, obviously not ready to drop it. "Do you mean that *Paige* turned *you* down?"

Pretty much. "Not exactly." He didn't need his hired help knowing he'd struck out. "It's complicated."

Lulu grabbed the gym keys off the table.

He flipped off the lights.

"Well, whatever the story is," she said, "have fun on your *hot* date."

Jack wasn't sure, but he thought he noted a hint of derision in her tone. Frowning slightly, he left her to lock up on her own.

Slinging his gym towel over his shoulder, he headed down the hall. He was Jack Banta, damn it. Successful resort owner, Hawaii's golden boy. And tonight, he had a hot…yes, he said it…a *hot* date. A date he'd waited for forever. And there was nothing, *nothing,* that was going to ruin it.

Tonight, he'd turn payback with Paige up a sensual degree.

Yep, that's right.

Jack strode through his grand resort, feeling better by the second.

Tonight was going to be good.

That evening, Paige stood outside Club Lealea's top-floor suite. Jack's suite. She took a calming breath and knocked on the door. Gosh, why was she so nervous?

Jack opened the door, and her breath caught in her throat. Oh, yeah, that was why. Could the man look any sexier? She reminded herself that she was only there to check out his bird book. Because, honestly, it wasn't really a date. She'd just said that to tick off Lulu, right?

From somewhere inside the suite, soft music floated into the air and drifted past Jack, gliding around his solid, muscular frame.

"Hi." He ran a lazy gaze down the length of her body, and his eyes glinted their approval. "Come on in."

Paige entered his foyer and glanced at Club Lealea's premier quarters. She mouthed a silent "wow". The floor plan was grand—open, airy, luxurious. Subdued lamplight caressed plush sofas and tickled the highlights in the artwork on the walls. Tropical trees in rich earthen planters adorned the far corners of the room.

Paige glanced at the floor-to-ceiling windows that opened to a balcony overlooking the sunset. White-capped waves bobbed along the ocean in the distance. "This is beautiful."

"I'm glad you like it. It's not much," he said with a grin. "But it's home. Come on in and make yourself comfortable." He sauntered over to the wet bar. "Wine?"

"Sure. Whatever you're having."

"Coming right up." He pulled two wineglasses out of the bottom cabinet, whistling beneath his breath along with the music.

Paige padded across the room, her sandals sinking into the plush carpet. She walked to the balcony windows and gazed at the ocean.

Jack strolled across the living room and handed a slender glass of white wine to her. "Here you go."

"Thanks." She took a sip.

He joined her at the window. "I've been hearing some interesting bird calls off the deck in the evenings."

"You have?"

"Yep. It's turning dark, but we might be able to hear them if we go out there before it gets too late."

"Oh, I'd like that." Intrigued, Paige followed him onto the massive deck that overlooked the ocean. Warm, lightly salted air met her as she stepped outside. She turned her face to the gentle breeze.

"The sun's about to go down, so I'm not sure we'll be able to spot anything," Jack said.

Paige glanced at the horizon where the sun was beginning its descent. "You have a beautiful view from up here."

He nodded. "The sunsets are great." He picked up a small, pocket-sized book off the deck table and handed it to her. "I bought this for you. Thought you might find it interesting."

Paige set her glass down and took the book. "*Birdcalls of Hawaii?* Jack, how nice of you." She stared back at him, touched by his thoughtfulness. And he was right. She *did* find it interesting. "This is perfect."

"It describes the different calls and what they mean—like mating calls versus distress signals. It even has a CD inside to listen to."

He gave her an easy smile, and her heart gave a soft little sigh in return. She swallowed. He looked perfect, too. Casual. Sexy.

He leaned one hand against the railing, and the wind kicked through his hair, ruffling it into disarray. Suddenly, he cocked his head. "Listen. There's the call." He turned and pointed to the left. "Hear it over there?"

Paige listened carefully. A birdcall rose up from the trees, a low, mournful summons. A second later, another bird answered from across the way.

"Have you ever heard that before?" he asked.

"No, I haven't." Curious, Paige reached for a pair of binoculars on the table and searched the surrounding trees. The evening light was fading fast. She squinted through the lens but couldn't spot the bird.

Another call came from the other end of the deck. She shifted her gaze toward the nearby trees and heard a flap of wings. But saw nothing. She lowered the binoculars. "I can't make them out. It's too dark. But it's a pretty call, don't you think? Lonely, drawn out."

Jack agreed.

She picked the book up and flipped through it, while Jack reached for the binoculars and took a look for himself.

"Night calls…" Paige murmured, reading the index, then turning to the section. She frowned down at the text. "Hmm, it says here it could be one of several birds, depending on the series of notes." She pondered the calls for a moment. "Would you say it was more of an ooo-oo, ooo-oo?" She turned the page and read further. "Or is it, woo-woo-hoo, woo-woo-hoo?"

Jack slowly lowered the binoculars and looked at her. She met his gaze, and in that instant she realized how dorky she'd just sounded.

His lips twitched.

So did hers.

They both began to laugh.

Paige was glad she felt comfortable enough to be herself around Jack. He'd known her well in school, and now he was getting to know her even better. And he seemed to like what he knew, quirks and all. The thought warmed her. Maybe more than it should.

She glanced across the open sea. Beyond the waves, the sun blew its parting kiss to the horizon, and the sky, in turn, blushed a shy shade of pink.

Jack's presence mingled with hers—close, together, the two of them alone on the deck. She liked the whiff of freshly showered soap that lingered on his skin. And she appreciated how he'd gone out of his way to find the bird book for her. It had been a thoughtful gesture. Absently, she rubbed her hands along her bare arms.

"Are you cold?" He slid his palm down the length of her arm, his warm fingers leaving a tingling trail of awareness along her flesh.

"Just a little."

"Let's go inside. It's too dark to see the birds now. I think they've left for the night."

"Okay." They returned to the living room, and Paige sank gratefully onto a sofa, still a bit worn-out from the exercise class that afternoon.

"Let me get the other book I was telling you about earlier," Jack said. He disappeared into another room and returned seconds later.

When he joined her on the sofa, the seat cushion sank beneath his weight.

Paige's senses stood on alert.

He was near enough for her to catch a trace of sea breeze that still clung to his clothes.

She busied her hands, taking a sip of wine. "That's quite a book. It's big."

"Yep. It lists the birds we might see on the tour and also explains bird behavior. Go ahead. Have a look."

She thumbed through it. "This is great. Sometimes it's hard to catch characteristics through the binoculars, but this—" she turned another page and perused the color photos "—this has beautiful detail." She squinted closer at a picture. "Maybe we'll see one of these birds. An Iiwi—the Hawaiian Honeycreeper. Says here they're rare." She read out loud, "'Disease, habitat loss and predators have made this native species scarce.' Oh, that's sad." She took a closer look at the photo. "Red on top, with black on the wings and a curved bill. It's a tiny little bird. Isn't it cute?" She turned the book toward Jack and paused.

He was smiling at her with an amused gleam in his eyes. It was an intimate look. A speculative look. As if he found her immensely entertaining. "Mmm, yes, very cute," he murmured. He kept his gaze trained on her, not glancing at the page. Her cheeks heated, and she looked away.

Beside the sofa, a spicy candle flickered its scent through the room. Its flame gave her a knowing wink as if sensing the flustered beat of her heart. She took another sip of wine and glanced around—anywhere but at Jack with those sensual blue eyes.

She straightened her blouse and refocused her attention on the bird book.

"Before you bury your nose too far into that guide," Jack said, "why don't we make a toast?"

She turned to him. "Oh. Okay. Sure."

He looked confident and entirely male, relaxing beside her on the sofa.

He opened his mouth to begin the toast, but before he said a word, she blurted out, "Here's to old friends."

He quirked an eyebrow, and a slow smile crept to his face. "Okay," he said easily. "To old friends." His masculine fingers cupped the glass. "And to new experiences." His last low words sent a stir racing along her spine.

Clink. He tapped his glass to hers and took a sip. His lips pressed against the crystal, his light blue eyes glittering at her over the rim—keen, assessing, seductive. His throat worked slowly as he swallowed.

Her mouth went dry.

The feelings he coaxed from her pulled Paige out of her comfort zone. She wished she didn't find him so sexy.

She closed her eyes for a brief moment and cursed the attraction she felt for this man. He wasn't her type.

She looked down at the bird book in her lap and flipped the page. "Mating Behavior." The chapter title caught her attention, and she raised the book closer to her nose, blocking out Jack's handsome, distracting face. She scanned a few paragraphs.

"Oh, look," she murmured. "Here's a bird that mates for life."

"No kidding?" Jack looped his forefinger over the top of the book and lowered it from in front of her nose. "Mind if I have a look?"

"Um, no, of course not." She gulped when he scooted closer.

He glanced at the page. "I didn't know there were birds that did that," he said.

All this talk of mating was making her increasingly

aware of the man next to her on the couch. His leg rested casually against hers. She clenched her knees together to keep from touching him further.

Jack scanned the page and chuckled. He read out loud, "'These birds go through courting rituals and date around for a while before engaging in a mutually exclusive partnership for life.'" He shook his head. "Interesting."

Paige studied him as he read the book, and a question came to mind. He had never mentioned any past girlfriends or relationships. She was sure he'd "dated around", but had Jack Banta ever been in love? Curious, she realized she wanted to know more.

"Speaking of mutually exclusive partnerships," she ventured, "have you…you know, ever been serious with anyone?"

He shrugged. "I've had girlfriends before, if that's what you mean. But nothing I'd ever call real serious."

She gave him a teasing smile. "So, no 'mating for life' for you?" She kept her tone light, but in reality she really wanted to know.

"You mean do I ever plan to marry someday?"

"Mmm-hmm."

He glanced up from the book and grinned. "Why? Are you proposing?"

The thought of being married to him made her heartbeat kick up a notch. Married…mating for life…the two of them entwined on their marital bed.

"I don't know about marriage," Jack answered. "I find it's best to keep things light and easy."

"So, you plan to 'fly solo' the rest of your life?"

He shrugged again and lowered his gaze to the wine-glass in his hands. "Yeah. Sure." A pensive look slipped across his features. "Maybe." He shifted on the couch. "Relationships are hard," he said softly after a moment. "People have a way of leaving. And sometimes—" he coughed, an odd, strangled sound "—and sometimes, it's just not worth it, you know?"

Paige paused and studied the quiet expression on his face. Typically, he kept his guard up when it came to anything resembling true feelings. Whenever a heavy topic arose, Jack seemed to change the subject or brush it off. But it appeared he'd let his guard down for a minute, and she wanted to grasp the sudden opportunity to delve beneath his usual fun-and-games exterior.

"When you say that people have a way of leaving," she said, "do you mean as in rejection? Like when someone breaks up with you?"

He ran a hand through his hair, leaving soft tufts in its wake. "That's one way." His eyes were brooding, and the lines softened along his forehead as he stared down at his glass.

At the word "rejection", her mind shifted back to the times she'd rejected him in school.

Heck, she hadn't meant to be rejecting, *per se*. She'd turned him down because she'd only liked him as a friend. She hadn't seen him in a romantic way. Besides, she'd been as shy and studious as he'd been. Having Jackson Banta as her boyfriend would only have made things worse for her. She'd been struggling to weather the social climate as the new girl in class. Dating the shyest boy in school hadn't been the way to go about it.

But, looking back, she felt bad for that fact. Because, in reality, Jackson had been the only person who had accepted her, right from the start. He'd become her study-buddy. Her staunch defender. Her friend.

Back then, she'd been immature. She'd gone with the flow, choosing to be like the others rather than date someone different, like Jack.

Had she grown out of that mindset these days? She'd like to think so. But, lately, she was realizing that she still let others choose things for her. Just look at how she'd allowed Aunt Naomi to send her to Club Lealea.

And that knowledge irked Paige. She was an adult now. Maybe it was high time to take some risks, stop simply reacting to things and start acting independently of others. Take charge, make her own decisions.

She gazed back at the man sitting next to her. Gone was the awkward Jackson Banta from the past. In his place was a man who was, well…who was confident. Attractive. Kind.

Suddenly, she remembered how Jack's father had abandoned him. And then how his beloved stepfather had died years later.

Maybe Jack found it hard to form attachments to others, she mused. Maybe he harbored a fear of rejection and couldn't picture a serious commitment with anyone because of how his loved ones had left him in the past.

Knowing all of that now made her feel guilty for how she'd turned him down back in school. If she'd known what he'd been through back then, maybe she would've found a way to soften her refusals to date him. Or maybe she'd have realized that image and popularity weren't all-important and would've given him a chance.

Paige felt a closeness to him in that moment. A closeness that had come from finally understanding more about him.

Without thinking, she reached up and gently touched his face.

CHAPTER SEVEN

PAIGE'S fingers felt soft and tentative against Jack's cheek. He hadn't planned on having a heavy conversation this evening, but he sure didn't mind her gentle touch.

What was it about women that made them want to talk about personal stuff—relationships, feelings? He shook his head. Leave it to Paige to turn his get-lucky sofa into a psychiatrist's couch.

He didn't like discussing emotions. It made him uncomfortable. Brought up feelings and memories he'd worked hard to leave far behind.

Paige seemed to be trying to delve beneath his surface. But women responded more readily to his carefree, bachelor persona, not the real man underneath. Why spoil the illusion?

"You know," she said quietly, "the only reason I didn't go out with you in school was because we were friends. I didn't think of our relationship in any other way."

Jack took the book from her hands and flipped through it. He didn't want to talk about this. Besides, he could read between the lines. The reason she hadn't seen him as anything other than a friend was because he'd been a skinny, nerdy kid. Not a hunk.

"I'm sorry if you felt rejected." She laid her hand on his knee. "I didn't know any better back then."

Uh-oh. The last thing he wanted was for her to feel sorry for him. That definitely wouldn't enhance the studly image he'd been trying to pull off.

He glanced down at the slender fingers resting on his leg. The heat from her palm melted through his khaki pants and warmed his skin. Hmm. On second thought, that wasn't bad. Not bad at all.

He tried to laugh things off. "That was years ago. We were kids. It would be pretty sad if I were still hung up on something that happened that long ago." But was he still hung up on it? Maybe. A little. It wasn't as if he dwelled on it every day—thinking how Paige Pipkin had rejected him in high school. He snorted at the idea. Then he frowned. On the other hand, when he really thought about it, he did hate rejection. Avoided it like the plague. Was that why he tended to keep things on the surface? Why he didn't put himself out there— didn't put his heart out there?

"You're right," Paige said, interrupting his musing. "That was a long time ago."

And there was that look again. The caring expression that made his heart turn over in his chest. Maybe there was something to this talking thing, after all.

A slight grin touched his lips, and he tried to recall another emotionally painful story he might rehash for her benefit. *Let's see, there was the time I broke my arm in sixth grade. Or the time I lost the go-cart race, because I didn't have a father to help me build the racer.*

Jack absently turned the next page of the book. "Courtship Rituals." Staring up at him was a color photo of a male bird, all puffed-up, displaying its plumage in grandiose style, its tail feathers fanned, chest extended.

Jack grinned softly and shook his head. Poor sap. All in the name of love. Or at least sex. The male bird strutted about like a pompous fool. Not much different than the men at the club, Jack realized. Swaggering around, shirtless and flexing, posturing for the ladies. Hell, when he really thought about it, he wasn't much different himself. He worked out at the gym, honing his physique. The grin that had started slowly faded from his lips. Come to think of it, wasn't that what his singles' clubs were all about? And wasn't that the life he'd chosen, as well? He'd dropped his geeky awkwardness, compensating with a new, suave, bachelor image. Much like the puffed-up bird, mocking him from the pages of his own book.

Jack snorted at the irony. Damn, males were idiots sometimes. Him included. He shook his head and smothered a chuckle at the bird's display. *Good luck with that, pal.* He hoped the bird would have better success than he was having with the female he'd been trying to impress all night.

He glanced at Paige. She was leaning toward him, reading about the courtship rituals, too.

God, she was attractive. Maybe not in the eyes of some, but to him her beauty lay in the simple lines of her face, in the inquisitive tilt to her head, and in the intelligence that lurked behind her eyes.

She was close to him as she peered at the book in his lap. And she smelled good—a subtle, pleasant mixture of ginger, shampoo and promise. His fingers itched to loosen her pony-tail, feel her silky black hair cascade through his hands.

"Hmm, listen to this," she said, reading out loud. "Female birds of this species initiate courtship rituals themselves. The female is the aggressor, seducing the male to her nest and engaging in…well, you can read the rest for yourself. It goes on about courtship dances and mating."

"Lucky males," Jack murmured, watching her. A gentle pulse beat rhythmically along the side of her throat. He'd like to sample that spot with his lips.

"You think the males are lucky?" She glanced at him. "I've heard that aggressive females can turn a guy off. I always thought men liked to do the courting."

"I guess it depends," he answered. "Some guys like to have a woman take the lead." He reached up and brushed a strand of hair from her face. She swallowed and flicked a glance at his mouth. Was she thinking about a kiss? He let his lips curve into a slow smile, and her expression wavered just enough to tell him that she was.

He tested his luck by running the tip of his finger along her cheek. She didn't flinch from his touch.

Heck, maybe the bird book had a point. Some females might do better if they were left in charge. To be the aggressor. Initiate "courtship rituals" themselves. Maybe that was the secret to getting past Paige's uptight exterior.

Piqued by the idea, Jack wondered how to entice her into making a move. "Let me ask you something," he said casually. "Have you ever been the aggressor before?"

"Who, me? With a man?" She let out a half laugh. "Uh, no."

"Why not?" He reached up and toyed with the clasp that held her pony-tail together.

"That's just not my, um, style." She frowned slightly as if the realization of what she'd just said bothered her.

"I'm betting it's not a matter of style," he replied, loving that her hair was soft and dark as night. "I'm betting that it's because you've never been brave enough to go for it."

She snorted unconvincingly. "What? I…I'm brave."

"Are you?" Before he knew it, he'd flicked her barrette open. Her hair tumbled loose like a long black waterfall, cascading across her shoulders.

She gasped. "Jack, what did you do that for?" Her silken strands flowed through his fingers, and she reached up to re-clasp the barrette.

"No," he murmured. "I like your hair this way. You should wear it down more often. There's nothing like hair that's left down. Just like this. It's…touchable."

"It is?"

"Definitely."

Paige watched Jack as he toyed with a strand of her hair. Why did knowing that he liked her hair please her so much?

She shifted on the sofa.

It definitely hadn't been a good idea to come to his suite. She'd known she was in trouble the second he'd sat next to her. He was far too attractive, and his nearness made her lose all concentration.

He was close enough for her to read the contour of his lips—every line, each crease of the fleshy curves that crooked into a slow grin. And suddenly she wanted to kiss him.

He'd said he didn't believe she was brave enough to make the first move, but with him next to her—warm, close, watching—she suddenly yearned to prove him wrong. Hadn't she just been thinking that it was time to take charge for once in her life? She was always reacting to things, rather than making things happen. And, suddenly, she wanted very much to make a kiss between them *happen*.

"Do you want to kiss me, Paige?" he asked softly.

She flicked a glance at his mouth. All she had to do was tilt her chin…lean forward a fraction of an inch. "Maybe." She swallowed. "Do you want me to?"

A slight smile creased the edges of his mouth. "Maybe."

She let out a snort that was supposed to say, *Then I'll wait till you're sure.* But instead it sounded more like, *Tell me more.*

She wasn't the type to initiate the kissing. The few men she'd kissed, she'd been on the receiving end. She stared back at him and found the promise of unspoken pleasures in his eyes. Pleasures she'd never known before. And, suddenly, she wanted to experience each and every one.

He was studying her quietly, inches away, as she pondered what to do. She really shouldn't.

Or should she?

Nope, she definitely would not.

But she did.

Before she knew it, she'd placed the palm of her hand against his cheek and lined her mouth up with his. The inch of space that hovered between their lips sparked with expectancy. Carefully, she leaned forward and pressed her lips to his. Her mouth trembled, and she felt the gentle give of his warm lips. Mmm, she liked this. Taking charge of the kiss emboldened her. It was a heady feeling, a new experience. He parted his lips, letting her proceed as she chose. She kissed him softly, then changed the angle.

She heard his quick intake of breath, and suddenly his arms were around her, drawing her close.

Paige lightly ran her hands over the sides of his face, slipping along the curve of his ear, and roaming along the rough, stubbled edge of his jaw.

She really shouldn't be doing this. But it felt right.

As if sensing her inner struggle, Jack deepened the kiss, teasing her with a finesse that excited her. He took over at that point, as if he'd waited patiently, and now it was his turn.

He tangled his fingers through her hair and pressed deeper against her lips. The moment she parted her mouth, she felt the heated yet gentle thrust of his tongue.

Her mind whirled with frenzied sensation. Stunned by her own behavior, she gave up and just went with the feeling, threading her fingers through his hair.

He shaped his mouth to hers and brought her closer to him, pressing his body against hers. He groaned softly and lowered her back against the sofa.

Oh, my. Suddenly, they were lying down, with him above her. The full length of his body molded to hers, and she found herself pressing back. She kissed him with fervor, and soon his hands drifted to the buttons of her blouse. Her breathing hitched as he reached for the top button and flicked it open. He dragged his lips from her mouth and paused, gazing down at her. When she didn't protest, he smiled slowly and unbuttoned the second button, then the third. He lowered his head and placed a soft kiss along the widening V of her shirt.

Paige shivered with anticipation. Though she wasn't a complete innocent, her experience was limited in the romance department. Caught up in the moment, she focused solely on Jack and his large, masculine hands. He flicked open her next button. Then the next. She felt her blouse sweep apart, and she sucked in a breath as his fingers brushed across her bare skin.

Thank goodness she'd bought a new bra and panties after gym class this afternoon. Not that she'd planned on having Jack actually *see* them this evening, but—

He slid a finger beneath the front clasp of her new bra, and with one flick he'd opened it.

Her eyes widened. Immediately self-conscious, she moved to cover herself, but Jack had already lowered his head, gently drawing her nipple into his mouth.

It felt excruciatingly arousing to have his mouth at

her breast, and she arched instinctively beneath him. A low murmur of pleasure escaped her throat.

Jack placed a soft kiss on one puckered tip, then moved to her other breast to claim its possession, as well.

Paige closed her eyes beneath a wave of pleasure, not believing she'd allowed this to happen. But it felt exhilarating to have Jack against her, touching her, kissing her.

Her dreamy gaze drifted to the long-forgotten bird book, lying on the coffee-table beside them. Slowly, she came to her senses, remembering what she'd come to Jack's suite for in the first place. To study birds—not writhe on the sofa beneath his gentle touch. *Half-naked, no less.* Paige squeezed her eyes shut and took a deep breath.

She hadn't meant to succumb to his charm.

Jack trailed kisses along Paige's collar-bone and up to her throat, loving every inch of her creamy, smooth skin. He'd been with other women before, but his feelings for Paige made each touch, every experience, feel brand new. He cupped her breast and felt its tip tighten beneath his fingers. She was perfect. Smooth, silky, and even better than he'd ever imagined.

And who knew she wore lacy pink bras beneath her frumpy clothing?

"Jack."

He groaned and brought her even closer in his arms. Was she asking him to stop? Or begging him to continue? He was beyond comprehending which.

Suddenly, Jack was struck with how long it had been

since he'd had a woman in his bed. He rose up and gazed at Paige beneath him on the couch. He liked the flush of her cheeks and her sexy, tousled hair.

Taking her to bed tonight hadn't been part of his plan. But the things this woman did to him… Hell, he couldn't think straight when he was with her. Normally, he was the one in control, and things always went the way he planned. But with Paige? His feelings and emotions were all over the map. One minute he wanted to take her to his bedroom and indulge in every fantasy known to man, and in the next minute he was terrified of where that might lead. Unsettled by his thoughts, he tried to shake off the feeling and lowered his mouth for another kiss.

But she slipped out from under him, and his pucker landed against the soft fabric of the sofa cushion.

Jack frowned. "Hey. Are you okay?"

Paige sat up, tugging her lacy bra back together. An embarrassed look stole across her face. "I'm fine. It's just that things went a little too far tonight, don't you think?"

"Too far?" He ran his fingers through his hair. "I wouldn't say they went *too* far." He smiled at her softly.

She snorted. "Well, I would." Her fingers fumbled with the last of her buttons. She picked up his big bird book. "We came here to go through this, and, instead, we ended up…"

He grinned, waiting for her to finish her sentence. She didn't. Jack decided he liked her with her color high and her hair messy. It was a side of her he'd never seen before, and he'd definitely like to see more. Initially, he'd meant for his plan to be simple. A little kiss, a little flirting. But he was finding himself wanting more…in every way.

That knowledge gave him pause.

Paige straightened the last of her clothing.

If Jack knew her as he thought he did, she'd probably been battling between her ever-present self-control and letting loose for once in her life. And, frankly, he was more than a little pleased with which one had won.

Paige, on the other hand, didn't look quite so pleased. He frowned, feeling bad for her. Her feelings mattered to him. Really mattered. He didn't want her to feel bad about kissing him. He handed her barrette to her.

She took it, cheeks flaming, and smoothed her hair back into its restrictive grasp.

He frowned. It wasn't as if they'd just had crazy, neighbor-waking, circus sex. She shouldn't be so hard on herself.

She tucked the small birdcall book with the CD into her purse and glanced at him. "So," she said, nodding at his other, larger book. "Do you mind if I take that with me tonight? I like to read in bed before I go to sleep."

"Sure." So, the only one getting her into bed tonight was his book. Figured. Jack felt the last hint of romance deflate from their evening. Flat and soured, like the last inch of wine that lingered in his glass.

He reluctantly followed her, *and his bird book*, to the door.

She turned to him at the entry. "It's been—" she flushed "—an interesting evening."

He chuckled. Interesting? Okay. He'd take that as a compliment…he guessed.

She headed through the doorway and into the hall.

"What? No goodnight kiss?"

She gave him a withering look.

He opened his mouth to speak, but she interrupted.

"I have to go." She fumbled with the book in her hands. "Thanks for the wine. And the birdcall book and CD, too." Her words were awkward, tumbling out of her mouth without pause. She took her room key out of her purse and dropped it on the floor.

Jack leaned down and picked it up. He handed it to her.

"Thanks." She opened her mouth and then shut it. Then opened it again. "Good, um, goodnight, then." She held her hand out for a shake.

Jack quirked an eyebrow and stared at her hand.

"Right," she said. "Um…" She patted his shoulder instead and gave him a jerky nod. With that, she clutched his book to her chest, turned and walked briskly down the hall, away from his suite.

Jack's lips twitched. Wow. That was…that was something. He'd been just about to point out that she'd buttoned her blouse all wrong.

Oh, well. He leaned against his door frame and watched the happy couple—Paige and his book—depart. It had been an interesting evening indeed. Jack smiled to himself and closed the door.

CHAPTER EIGHT

THE NEXT day, Jack stepped out of his office and took a look around the club's lobby. He hadn't seen Paige since she'd left his suite the night before. But he could still feel her soft flesh beneath his hands. He smiled softly, remembering the way she'd kissed him with that inexpert charm—her kisses turning passionate, less controlled later on. It was enough to make a man hard just thinking of it.

He gazed around the bustling hotel lobby. The resort was busy.

The front-desk clerk was on the phone, while four guests stood in line, waiting to register. To help his frazzled employee, Jack answered the next phone call that came in.

He held the receiver between his shoulder and ear, leaving his hands free to take a message. As he took the call he watched two female senior citizens enter through the club's revolving doors. The frizzy-redheaded woman walked through the foyer, but her shorter companion got caught up in the revolving doors and wound up back outside. She tried again, and this time her friend latched on to her arm and ushered her inside.

The two elderly women stood there, gawking at the place.

Just then, a group of young men in swim trunks sauntered by. The redhead slid her sunglasses down her nose and ogled their backsides over the rim of her glasses. Her bright lipstick-covered lips formed a wolf-whistle that echoed through the Lealea lobby.

Good Lord. Jack hung up the phone and watched in fascination as the odd duo checked out his resort.

The tall redhead strutted around in a pair of the loudest floral shorts he'd ever seen, accompanied by a green cleavage-baring tube top that looked oddly out of place on a woman her age. Her shorter companion tottered after her, assisted by a long metal cane with a four-pronged bottom. She wore a white and purple muumuu that looked much too large for her wizened frame.

Jack shook his head, wondering what hare-brained marketing plan his assistant manager Nick had come up with recently to attract this particular demographic. His curiosity piqued, he left the check-in counter and walked up behind them as they looked out the windows at the pool.

"Hoo-wee," Green Tube Top said, nudging her elbow into the shorter one's side. "You got a swimsuit with you?"

"A-hem." Jack cleared his throat behind them.

They turned.

"Morning, ladies," he said politely, gracing them

with his best resort-host smile. "I'm Jack, the host and owner. Welcome to Club Lealea." He sounded like Mr Roarke, welcoming them to Fantasy Island. Images of Tattoo flickered through his mind, and he coughed behind his hand, trying again. "I, uh, don't see any bags with you. Did you leave them with the bellboy? Because I'd be happy to check you in to our club, if you're ready."

Green Tube Top stuffed her sunglasses in her pocket and tucked a lock of frizzy orange curls behind her ear. She grinned beneath her leathery tan. "Oh, no. We're not staying at the resort. We're just here to visit a guest."

She ran her eyes slowly down the length of his body and back up again, leaving Jack feeling naked. He swallowed a strangled sound.

"Maybe you've met my niece," the woman continued. "Paige Pipkin?" She winked at him. "If you haven't met her...I'll make sure you do. She could use an introduction to a fine young man like yourself."

A smile started slowly across Jack's face, then spread. So, this was Aunt Naomi. Who'd have thought it? She was the screaming opposite of her conservative niece. He chuckled softly and held out his hand. "Ms Pipkin, is it? It's *very* nice to meet you."

She shook his hand and glanced around as if making sure no one was listening. "Just call me Naomi. Ms Pipkin makes me sound old, and I need all the help I can get at a swinging singles' place like this."

Yes. She did. "Naomi it is." He grinned at her. "And I *have* met Paige. We went to school together here on Kauai. She's told me all about you." He leaned closer and lowered his voice to a teasing level. "But between you and me, she forgot to mention what a looker you are." He wiggled his eyebrows for her benefit.

"What?" her shorter friend chirped up at her side, adjusting her hearing-aid. "Did he say 'what a hooker you are'?"

"No, Irene. He said looker." Aunt Naomi gave him a saucy smile, then aimed a loud voice directly into Irene's ear. "The young man thinks I'm a fox!"

"Oh-h-h." Irene jiggled her hearing-aid with her finger. The ear-piece screeched, then fell silent. "Ah-h-h, that's better."

Jack grinned at the amusing pair. "So, you're not staying at our club?"

"No." Aunt Naomi shook her head, her plastic palm tree earrings swinging gaily beneath her ears. "Irene lives here on the island," she said. "We used to be neighbors when I taught junior high on Kauai, years ago. I'm staying at her house."

"Oh." For some reason, Jack felt disappointed that they weren't sticking around. He wouldn't mind spending some time with the entertaining duo. Besides, he could probably learn more about Paige from her aunt. Before he knew it, he found himself saying, "Hey, ah, why don't you two stay here at the club? My treat."

"What did he say?" Irene asked Naomi.

"He asked if we'd like to get a room here," Naomi hollered back.

"For the three of us?" Irene put her hands on her hips. "They move fast at these singles' resorts, don't they?"

She cocked her head and checked Jack out, making a full circle around him. "Eh—" she shrugged her skinny shoulders "—what the heck?"

"Gee, thanks for the ringing endorsement," Jack said. "But, ah, I meant a room for just the two of you."

"*Oh.*" Irene waved a dismissive hand. "I can't afford a room in a fancy-schmancy place like this."

"It would be on the house," Jack assured her. He gazed at her gray hair, teased high into a teetering mound atop her head. Good Lord, she was more hair than woman.

Just then, Paige exited the elevator. "Aunt Naomi!" She hurried through the lobby, a thrilled smile on her face, and was caught up in a giant hug by her aunt.

Jack felt a pull of emotion, deep in his gut, at the affection they clearly felt for one another. He'd never seen Paige so excited. He smiled softly as niece and aunt clasped each other tightly and rocked back and forth. Heck, he wished he could earn that happy smile from Paige himself.

"Mmm! Mmm! It's so good to see you." Aunt Naomi held her niece away from her. "Look at you." She beamed. "You look fantastic, honey." She lifted a tress of Paige's long black hair and quirked an eyebrow at her. "What's this? You're wearing your hair down, now?"

Paige flicked a glance at Jack and reddened. "Oh, you know." She shrugged. "Just trying something new."

Well, well. Jack rocked back on his heels. So, she was wearing her hair down now? After he'd told her he liked it that way? Interesting. More pleased than he should be, he listened as the two women caught up.

"And you're starting to get some color to you," Aunt Naomi was saying, running her hand along her niece's bare arm. "Been spending time at the pool?"

Paige nodded.

A thoughtful look flickered across Aunt Naomi's face. "Could it be you're actually having a good time here?" The merry twinkle in Naomi's eyes made it clear she approved of what she saw.

She turned to Jack. "It seems my niece is flourishing in your hands."

Jack watched Paige's eyes widen at her aunt's choice of words. His lips twitched. "Well, I do my best."

Paige ignored his wink.

"So, Paige," he said. "I was just offering your aunt and Irene a room here at the club. Free of charge. After all, your aunt flew all the way here to see you. You'll have more time together if she stays on site."

"Really? You'd do that?"

"Absolutely. They can stay as long as they'd like."

Paige's gaze collided with his…and lingered. A soft, grateful smile tilted her lips, and she turned to her aunt. "What do you say? That would be great, don't you think?"

"Hmm?" Aunt Naomi pulled her eyes off a young, muscle-bound stud on his way to the pool. She shook her head as if to clear it of the fantasy she'd been indulging. "Um, yes, I'd *love* to stay here. This is quite the place." She gave her niece an impressed nudge. Then her brows lowered a fraction. "But I didn't bring my bikini."

She tapped her chin and turned to Jack. "Do you sell bikinis here? Maybe one of those thongs that are popular these days?"

He laughed and ran his hand along his jaw. "Yeah. Yeah, we do."

Jack enjoyed the look on Paige's face. It was a blend of horror mixed with love for her aunt, as well as patient forbearance. Having her aunt on the property was going to be fun.

Paige put her arm around Naomi, giving her a quick squeeze. "Okay. Let's get you and Irene all settled, then." She turned and surprised Jack with a brief, impromptu hug. "Thanks for inviting them to stay," she said softly in his ear. "It means a lot to me."

Her breasts pressed momentarily against his chest, and then she released him. He composed himself and smiled. "Of course. I'm glad to do it." And he meant that. For some reason, it pleased him to see her happy.

When he glanced at Aunt Naomi, he found her watching him with a speculative gaze. A knowing look twisted through her eagle-sharp eyes, and a slow smile pulled at the corners of her mouth.

Jack gulped. *Naomi knew. She'd seen right through him.* Damn. Since when had he become so transparent?

He paused and slowly toyed with the knowledge. Maybe it wouldn't hurt to have a crafty ol' bird like Aunt Naomi on his side, after all, he mused.

And with the bird-watching tour scheduled tomorrow, he could begin the next phase of his seduction.

* * *

The next day, Jack paused at a clearing along the humid jungle valley and waited for Paige to catch up. They had veered off the trail, away from the others in the bird-watching group, because Paige thought she'd spotted her elusive Honeycreeper.

Not that Jack minded a bit. He'd been hoping to ditch the others anyway.

Paige ducked beneath a low-hanging vine and came to a stop by his side. She breathed hard from exertion. "Did you find it?" she asked, her green eyes bright with excitement.

"I thought I did, but I lost him. He flew that direction." Jack pointed across the grasses along the clearing. Coconut palm trees and dense forest brush enclosed the small valley, their tropical spires creating a leafy skyline in the distance. It was impossible to see the tiny bird now, from this far away.

She lifted the binoculars that hung from her neck and studied the grove of trees across the valley. "Hmm, I don't see him." After a moment of searching, she gave up. "Well, maybe there are more where he came from. Let's go back to where we first spotted him."

Jack smiled. "Okay, sure." He followed her back beneath the shade of the jungle.

Paige paused. "Oh, look," she whispered. "There's a bird in that bush. See it?" She lifted her binoculars. "It's not a Honeycreeper, though." She handed the binoculars to him.

Jack put them on and squinted at the shrub. Its drooping limbs sprouted skyward before cascading down to brush the ground. All he made out was a speck on one of the limbs, but Paige seemed excited.

"Can I get into my backpack?" she asked.

"Sure." He shrugged off the straps of the over-stuffed pack he'd offered to carry.

She rummaged around, setting aside sunscreen, note-pads, pens, and a floppy hat, before pulling out a book.

Jack squinted at the title. *Bird Classifications for the Backyard Ornithologist*. His lips twisted into a smirk. God, she really was cute.

She pointed at a picture and turned the book toward him. "I think that's what we've got over there."

"Ah." He was more interested in her than he was in the birds. He enjoyed watching her work.

"Oh, there's another one!" She grabbed the binoculars that still hung from his neck, jerking Jack along with her. She peered at the bird.

"Here, hold on." Jack contorted himself, looping his head out from the binocular straps, letting her have them all to herself.

She grabbed a pen from her backpack, opened a booklet, and started writing.

"What is that?" he asked.

"Hmm? Oh, it's my lifetime bird list." She turned the chart toward him. "You're supposed to mark every bird you spot over the years." She angled a look at him. "You really should start one. Today is a perfect day to begin your own list. I could help you if you'd like."

"Oh." Jack rubbed the side of his neck where the binocular strap had all but strangled him. "That's all right. We can just go with yours for now."

She shrugged. "Okay." She tucked her pen and the bird chart back in her bag.

They took a few more steps before Paige paused again and lifted the binoculars.

Jack took the moment to study the "ornithologist" at his side. Her slender arms crooked at the elbows, binoculars clutched in her hands as she searched through foliage and branches. Though they were alone, the forest around them hummed with sound. The distant squawk of a tropical bird, the hiss of insects hidden beneath leaves, the rustle of wind through the treetop canopy that lorded over the jungle below.

Jack breathed in the motionless air that hung heavy among the trees—vibrant, earthy, alive, mixed with the smell of ripe, rotting vegetation that seeped from the marshy underbrush.

Paige took a few steps ahead of him.

Jack moved his eyes along the graceful curve of her legs beneath her khaki shorts and up to the rounded slope of her backside. Soft curves. The kind of fleshy curves that would mold gently to a man's palm. Her thighs were flawless, too. Smooth, toned—perfect to ease between. His imagination took hold, and he pictured the two of them together—a gentle squeeze, a whispered moan. *Good Lord.* That whispered moan had just come from his throat.

"Did you say something?" she asked, binoculars glued to her eyes, not turning around.

Jolted from his daydream, he was just about to say no, when— "Ho-bajeez! Uh, Paige? Listen to me." He froze. "Do. Not. Move."

She paused, not turning around. "What?"

A spider, large enough to make a grown man wet himself, crawled along the back of her shirt.

Jack reached for a philodendron leaf from the ground, hoping to slide the spider onto it and away from Paige. He spied an even larger leaf and picked that one up instead.

"Jack, what is it? Why am I not moving like this?"

"Hold still," he said, not wanting to alarm her. "There's just a little something on the back of your shirt. Don't worry, I'm going to get it."

She slowly turned her head and glanced over her shoulder. "Oh, my, look at that." She tugged the collar of her shirt, dragging the spider toward her, until he crawled onto her palm.

"Paige! Are you nuts?"

"Oh, Jack." She smiled. "This little guy doesn't bite."

Little guy?

"He's actually beneficial against pestilent insects," she said, naming its genus and species. "See? He's just hungry for bugs."

Jack craned his neck for a better peek. The thing looked bloodthirsty, if you asked him.

"Want to hold it?" She took two steps toward him.

He took two steps back. "No, no. I'm good." He wondered if it would appear unmanly to shriek and run back to the tour bus. He glanced at the leaf in his hand— the size of an elephant's ear—and dropped it sheepishly.

Paige set the spider loose on a fern frond.

The hairy critter took a few creepy steps forward, then scooted to the underside of the frond, disappearing from view.

When Paige wasn't looking, Jack glanced at his own back. Blissfully spider-free, he shook out his shirt for good measure and rejoined her in her bird-hunt.

Together, they shuffled through the underbrush and treaded over gnarled tree roots. Meanwhile, Jack's mind trudged back to the conversation they'd had in his suite two nights earlier. Paige had wondered if fear of rejection had kept him from having a serious relationship.

Her words had made him think, and he had a sneaking suspicion she might be right. He frowned slowly. Hell, he didn't like delving into feelings, past hurts. He'd been extremely uncomfortable that night on the sofa. But not for the entire night. His lips twisted into a healthy grin. The evening might have started on a sour note for him, but it had ended very sweet. His healthy grin widened. Very sweet indeed.

But though they'd talked a lot about him that night, he suddenly realized they hadn't discussed anything about *her*. His smile faded. And the more time he spent with her, the more he'd grown curious. Had Paige ever been in love? Surely she'd had a boyfriend or two. Or had she? Did the bookish Ph.D. student make time for men in her life outside her university classes?

Pondering the question, he pushed his way through twisted foliage to find Paige at a clearing in the sun, where she'd stopped to study another bird.

She lowered her binoculars and grinned. She'd worn her hair down again, letting it glide softly about her shoulders. Since arriving at Lealea, her pale skin had tanned to golden brown and complemented the earthy hues that flickered in her eyes. "This has been great," she said. "I've spotted three new birds, and look." She pointed off to the side. "I think we've found the trail again. I'm sure the others are just up ahead."

Damn. "Great." He glanced toward the empty trail. At least they'd have a reprieve from the others for a little while longer.

"You know, I was thinking," Jack said, clearing his throat. "When we talked about past relationships the other night, you never said much about yours. What gives?" He grinned in an offhanded way, but, deep down, he actually cared about her past. Why? He wasn't sure. But still, he was curious.

She lifted a shoulder. "I had one serious boyfriend. Back in grad school."

The knowledge hit Jack like a punch in the gut. Surprised by his reaction, he swallowed. So, it was true. Paige had been in love, at least once. Someone had held her in his arms as Jack had the other night, touching her, kissing her… He refused to think what had come after that.

He paused. What was wrong with him? Of course she'd had men in her life. The woman wasn't a nun.

She shaded her forehead against the sun. "Yep. Just one serious boyfriend. Years ago." She angled a glance at him. "Unlike you, I prefer monogamy rather than flitting from partner to partner."

Jack leaned his head back and laughed. "Flitting from partner to partner? I guess that's one way to put it."

She frowned. "It's true, though, isn't it? I mean, look at all the women at your clubs. I've witnessed a few coming on to you. Are you telling me you don't, you know, accept an invitation now and then?"

Jack glanced down at his hiking boots and nudged at a twisted tree root sticking out from the dirt. Yeah, he could see how it might look as if he were a player. It came with the singles' business.

And, sure, he could score a heck of a lot more than he did. If he tried. But sometimes the illusion was more fun than the reality. The truth was— "I fooled around a bit in the beginning," he admitted. "Accepted a few 'invitations', as you put it, back when I started my first club. But now…" He shrugged.

She was listening to him quietly, taking in his words.

Jack shoved his hands in his pockets. He'd worked hard to build his new persona—Hawaii's most eligible resort owner, the guy who exuded allure and appeal, living the life of the free and easy. Did he really want to expose the man underneath? Admit that he wasn't quite the ladies' man that everyone assumed he was?

So far, his playboy act hadn't worked on Paige. Maybe it was time to set the record straight.

He gulped around his discomfort and decided to take the risk. "Listen, people take one look at my clubs, the singles' business as a whole, and just assume that I have this wild life. But the truth is…" He paused. "The truth is, I don't mess around with the women at my clubs like you'd think."

Paige tilted her head. "You don't?"

"No. That's not my style. I mean, I'm not a saint, by a long shot. But you'd be surprised. Besides, I want repeat customers. Getting involved in messy relationships won't achieve that goal." He dragged his hand through his hair. He'd be hard-pressed to remember the last time he'd actually bedded a woman. He glanced at Paige and rubbed his jaw. Far, far too long. "Let's just say that harmless flirting is what keeps most of my customers happy. That's really what it's all about."

There. He'd said it. Jack Banta wasn't the Casanova he'd been made out to be.

He studied her closely, waiting to see disillusion darken her eyes. The subtle let-down. The realization that he was just the same guy she used to know. Not a superstud.

A smile started slowly, then clung to Paige's lips. Well, who would've guessed that Jack Banta wasn't the player she'd thought he was? She felt a measure of admiration sneak through her chest as she stared back at him. She'd misjudged the attractive resort owner.

"I respect that, Jack. I guess I jumped to the conclusion, just like everyone else."

He looked surprised by her answer. And for some reason, knowing that women threw themselves at Jack without his rising to the occasion, so to speak, made her more attracted to him than ever.

He studied her intently through the bright sunlight, and he seemed to relax, as if relieved. His easygoing smile resurfaced, creasing the edges of his lips and high-lighting his eyes, making him look years younger.

"So, tell me about this one serious boyfriend you had in the past." His tone sounded casual now, more laid-back.

Paige brushed at a speck on the lens of her binoculars. She hadn't thought about her ex-boyfriend in a long, long time. "We were together for a year. But then he received a grant to study astrophysics in New York and—"

"Your one serious boyfriend was an *astrophysicist?*"

"Yes." She frowned. "What's wrong with that?"

"Nothing." The teasing light returned to his eyes, and his lips curved. "I just can't picture having fun with an astrophysicist."

"What? He…he was fun." Her answer sounded un-convincing, even to her.

"Was he?" Jack looked skeptical.

Why did guys always try to belittle other guys when they felt a hint of competition? "Mmm-hmm, lots of fun," she repeated.

"Oh, yeah?" Jack chuckled and shook his head. "Even in bed?"

Her mouth dropped open. She snapped it shut and crossed her arms. "The details of our intimacy are cer-tainly none of your business."

"Well, tell me this. Did your astrophysicist take you to the stars and back? Or was it over like a comet?"

A smile tugged at her mouth. Darn it, she wasn't going to give him the satisfaction of laughing at his joke.

"Or maybe you were only with him for his Big Dipper?" Jack quirked his head. "Or was it Little?"

"Are you finished?"

"Not yet. So, why did you two break up? Was he being an ass-troid?" He leaned his head back, and his good-natured laugh filled the air.

Paige swallowed a smirk.

Jack sobered and said, "Okay. Now, I'm done."

"As I was saying—" she gave him a pointed look "—Milton was a very interesting person. I found him intellectually stimulating as well as—"

"His name was *Milton?*"

She pursed her lips. "Yes, his name was *Milton.*"

"I'm sorry, but I just can't picture you rolling around in the sack, having loads of fun with an astrophysicist named Milton."

She huffed out a breath. "For your information, my experience with Milton was…" She paused, her mind flying back to the one and only time she'd slept with him before he'd moved to New York. She'd been quite sure it was his first time, too—the awkward fumblings, the uncomfortable weight of his body on top of her. "Highly satisfying," she finished.

"Really?" Jack said, grinning. "Care to elaborate?"

"I most certainly would not. But let's just say I wouldn't mind going out with another astrophysicist should one ever come along." What? Now, where had that come from?

Jack's teasing grin faded. "So, was this guy—" he shifted in his stance "—was this guy the love of your life?"

"I wouldn't exactly say that." Paige had fooled

herself into believing that she'd been in love with Milton. But, really, they'd felt more like friends. Dating him had been…comfortable. She frowned, realizing once again how she'd chosen the easy path. The comfortable guy. Sticking with Milton because he'd been, well, *there*. Not much of a risk. And certainly less reward. Because shouldn't it have been harder to say goodbye to him? If it had been true love—deep, real, long-lasting love—wouldn't they have ended up together in the long run? That was how she'd always pictured true love to be. That was what she secretly longed for but was too afraid to pursue.

Jack stepped closer to her, crowding her space, and she felt heightened prickles of awareness rise along her skin. He lowered his voice to a sensual level. "So, you miss all that highly satisfying sex, do you?"

She opened her mouth to reply, but when Jack's slow, sexy gaze shifted to her lips her words scattered from her mind like bougainvillea petals tossed about on the island breeze.

He reached up and slowly ran his finger along the binocular strap that lay against her throat. Her flesh tingled beneath his touch. "So, did your astrophysicist ever kiss you here?" Gently, he slipped the leather strap to the side and lowered his lips to her throat.

No. She gulped. She couldn't recall Milton ever kissing her there. Her senses leapt in instant response to Jack's touch, and her pulse thickened beneath his mouth.

"How about here?" he whispered, kissing her behind her ear.

Nope. Not there, either. She shivered. His warm lips felt thrilling, unnerving against her flesh.

"Did good ol' Milty ever do this?" He looped his finger beneath the strap and slowly traced it downward along the V of her cotton shirt. His eyes darkened as he followed the strap lower…and lower.

Paige stood perfectly still, transfixed in odd fascination by the tickle of his finger along her chest. She closed her eyes and swallowed.

CHAPTER NINE

JACK traced along the soft swell of Paige's breast and felt a tightening in his loins.

She was soft. Tempting.

He shifted his gaze to her face and found her eyes closed.

She looked beautiful standing before him, her dark lashes fanned against her sun-kissed skin.

He'd hated hearing about her damn ex-boyfriend, Milton. And he planned to put that guy out of her mind for the rest of the afternoon, if not for good.

She raised her lashes slowly and looked up at him. Awareness mingled with the brown highlights that flashed in her green eyes.

He had to kiss her—now. He brushed his thumb over her soft, parted lips and slowly lowered his mouth.

Her eyes widened.

Thrilled by her seeming eagerness for his kiss, he closed his eyes and…

His pucker went unanswered.

Jack opened his eyes to find Paige pointing to a spot behind him.

"Oh, my gosh! Look!"

He glanced over his shoulder.

She pointed to a tree that draped across the hiking trail. "That's it! An Iiwi, the Honeycreeper!"

Jack turned and looked at the tree. There, nestled among the branches, perched a tiny red bird.

Paige let out a breath of reverence. She lifted her binoculars. "Yep, curved beak, black on the wings. And did you hear that squeak he just made?" She spoke in a hushed voice as if not to frighten it.

Jack squinted at the bird, none too pleased by its untimely appearance. He glanced back at Paige and considered her profile as she gazed through her binoculars.

"It's pretty in a delicate way, don't you think?" she asked.

He moved his eyes along her cheek and over the full length of her hair, the ends curling at the tips. "Sure is," he murmured.

Just then, Lulu came tromping down the trail, along with two other hikers. "There you guys are!"

The Honeycreeper flapped at the commotion and flew out of the tree, disappearing above the jungle canopy.

Paige slowly lowered her binoculars. She swore softly.

Jack noted the disappointment that snaked through her gaze. She'd been waiting all day to locate that bird.

Lulu walked up to them. "We lost you guys a ways back. What've you been up to?"

The rest of the group ambled down the trail toward

them, entering the area, some stopping and looking around, others edging past them and continuing down the trail.

"Well, we were looking at an Iiwi, until he flew away, just now," Paige said.

Lulu spared Paige a glance. "Oh, really? That's a shame," she said flatly. She looked at Jack. "Since when did you become a big bird-watcher? This is the first time you've joined this tour."

"I like birds. Thought it sounded interesting."

"Hmm." Her eyes narrowed slightly, and she glanced back and forth between him and Paige. "Never heard of an Iiwi," she said to Paige.

"They're scarce these days."

"Oh." Lulu shrugged. "We saw the usual birds. Nothing fancy. Plus a few wild chickens." She turned to Jack. "So, you ready to head back to the bus?" She motioned toward the trail.

"Uh, yeah. We'll be down in a second." He wanted to talk to Paige. Alone.

"Oh. Okay." Lulu adjusted her bag. "I'll save you a seat on the bus." She smiled sweetly at him, then glanced at Paige. "See ya." With that, she turned and joined the others heading down the trail.

"Talk about bad timing," Jack said to Paige. "Too bad they scared off your bird."

"Yeah, it really is." She sighed. "I wanted a longer look at him before he flew off."

"Listen, a buddy of mine bought some forest land a while back. As an investment. He showed it to me before he bought it, and I remember seeing a ton of birds there. If you'd like, I could take you there tomorrow to see what we can find. I know he wouldn't mind. It's a nice piece of property. Not many people know of the area, so it's fairly secluded. It even has a river through it."

"Really?" Paige looked up at him, slowly nodding. "Sure. That…that would be great. I don't have much planned for tomorrow, other than spending some time with Aunt Naomi." She grinned. "I'll bring my bird list. Oh, and a camera."

"Great." Jack was pleased by his impromptu idea. It was a perfect way to spend time with Paige, away from the tours and interruptions. And he really did think they'd find some good birds for her to check out. The place was perfect. Tree-covered, secluded…romantic, actually, when he thought about it.

She only had one week left at his club. One week left for him to give her a taste of what she'd rejected all those years ago. Leave her at the end of her trip…wanting more.

Yep. He planned to send Paige home with a smile on her face and a new image of Jack Banta in her mind. *Check.*

A ridiculous grin spread across his lips at the thought. He couldn't help it.

"You know," Paige said. "Maybe Aunt Naomi would like to join us tomorrow."

Jack's smile faded.

The next day, Aunt Naomi peered up at Jack from beneath the shade of a patio umbrella. "Aloha, handsome. Come join us."

He took a seat beside Paige at their poolside table. "So," he said. "What have you ladies been up to all morning?"

Paige smiled. "Well, let's see. Aunt Naomi, Irene and I took a walk along the beach. Then we spent a few hours shopping. And we had a nice lunch in Princeville."

"And now I hear you've planned a hike this afternoon to look for birds?" Aunt Naomi asked him.

"Yep." He nodded.

She glanced at him speculatively and toyed with the curvy red straw sticking out of her frozen cocktail. She cocked an eyebrow. "A big birder, are you?"

Uh, no. "Uh, sure. I love birds."

"Mmm-hmm." Aunt Naomi adjusted the neon-green bikini straps of what must be her new swimsuit. "Well, you two kids have fun. I'm thinking about staying here and enjoying the pool. I'm sure you'll be just fine without me." Her "go-get-'em-tiger" smile told Jack she knew exactly what he was up to.

And, frankly, he didn't care. Each day that Paige spent at his club, he found his thoughts drifting to her, wondering what she was doing, when he would see her again. He received an unexpected jolt each time he caught a glimpse of her passing through the lobby or strolling past the pool.

When he really thought about it, that had *not* been part of his payback plan—falling for her all over again. In fact, he was treading on dangerous territory. Because the more he instigated his plan, the more he, himself, was yearning for *her*. He frowned slightly. He liked having her around, damn it. But at least the kiss they'd shared in his suite had left him with no doubt that she liked being around him, too. She might try to deny it, pretend she didn't like the feel of his hands on her warm, bare skin, but he knew otherwise. Just looking at her now, and thinking of spending the rest of the afternoon alone with her, putting a wrinkle or two in her neatly pressed outfit, brought a curve to his lips and a tightening in his groin—a condition he'd found himself in more and more often with Paige around.

Never had a woman tested his restraint as she did.

"Yoo-hoo!" A woman's voice drifted over the patio from the pool.

They turned in their seats to find Irene waving from the water. Aunt Naomi's shriveled little friend bobbed up and down in the shallow end. Enormous, bright-colored floaties encircled her arms, keeping her above the water. "Come on in, Naomi. The water's great!" She splashed her way to an abandoned pool-mattress and struggled aboard. Once on top, she stretched her skinny legs out in front of her and reached up into her teased nest of hair, pulling out a pair of sunglasses.

Just then, a muscle-bound hunk walked past the table, two of his buddies in tow. Aunt Naomi followed them with her eyes to the deep end of the pool, where they cannonballed into the water.

She raised an eyebrow. "Well, my mind's made up. I'm definitely staying here, because the pool just got a little more interesting." She rose and untied the sarong from around her waist. "You two have fun on your outing." With that, she dropped her sarong on her empty chair. "Oh, boys!" She waved to them. "Anyone up for pool-volleyball?" She bent to grab a volleyball, then headed for the water.

Jack gaped at her thong-bared bottom. A flower tattoo winked out at him from one wrinkled, fleshy cheek.

He glanced at Paige.

"Yeah." She sighed. "I know."

After hiking for over an hour, Paige paused and took a moment to catch her breath. So far, she and Jack had spotted five species of birds on his friend's remote jungle property, as well as a wild boar and a free-range goat.

Jack caught up and stopped beside her.

"You were right," she said, smiling. "This place is perfect." She was having a good time, and it was all because of him.

Overhead, the sun trickled through the canopy of trees, its dappled light playing hide-and-seek through the leaves.

"There's a waterfall here, too," Jack said.

"Really?"

"Yep. It's a bit of a hike, but we can go see it, if you'd like."

"I'd love to."

"Great. It's this way." He took the lead.

They hiked over grasses, past ferns and sprawling foliage. Eventually the area became marshy, with gentle streams of water trickling past black rocks and edging around expansive tropical plants.

Paige followed Jack, watching his well-toned legs as he walked. He moved with a subtle grace that she'd grown accustomed to. She smiled with something deeper than desire—honest affection, she realized, thinking how his carefree attitude and gentle teasing made her life feel more exciting. It was one of the many things she'd come to love about him.

She paused suddenly, brought up short by the thought. The things she'd come to *love*? Was she falling in love with Jack?

He continued, and she followed him more slowly now, her mind working along with her footsteps. She'd changed since she'd arrived at his club. For once in her life, she was starting to feel more relaxed, more confident, and she'd definitely let her hair down a bit. Heat crept to her cheeks, as she recalled how her evening had ended in Jack's suite on his sofa. *Letting my hair down, indeed.*

Her mind shifted to the kindness Jack had shown toward her aunt and Irene while they'd been at his club. That had pleased her more than she could ever express. Paige smiled softly. Jack made her feel… alive. Invigorated.

The roar of the waterfall grew more distinct as they neared, pulling Paige from her thoughts. She followed Jack, and soon they reached a solid wall of lava rock that loomed straight up before them. A few steps later, they broke through the vines and trees and entered a clearing next to the base of the falls.

A narrow river of water dropped over the edge of the cliff above them. Paige breathed out softly. "Oh, it's beautiful." The air settled thick and steamy in the area, a few degrees cooler than the neighboring jungle forest.

"You like it?" Jack asked.

"Like it? It's stunning." A smattering of large moss-covered rocks rested upon the sandy ground, encircled by lush plants and trees, creating a natural alcove. Drops of moisture pooled on the bright green foliage, the plants luxuriating in the misty botanical paradise.

Shoulder to shoulder, she and Jack stepped out of the shade and walked to the water's edge. The waterfall kept up a constant chatter, bubbling over its rocky ledge and splashing into the pool below. Beneath the falls, the water roiled, passionate and foamy, before settling down and drifting into clear, swirling pools that floated calmly past them, and then gathering speed once again to flow downstream.

"You'd never guess this place even exists from over in the valley," Paige said. "Is the water warm?"

"Why don't you feel it and see?"

"Great idea." She sat on a rock and took off her hiking boots and socks. Then she padded barefoot to the water's edge. The sandy earth felt cool beneath her feet. "Mmm, it's perfect. Feels good after the hike." She waded further until the water banked against her calves below her shorts.

Jack took his shoes off, too, and waded in to join her.

She glanced at the towering cliff wall. "Don't you love the volcanic rock of the island?" she murmured. "I love the contrast of black lava rock against the light sand." She shifted her gaze to Jack and found him staring down at her, his blue eyes intense.

He simply nodded in answer. After a moment of

silence, he asked, "You know who the goddess of the volcano is, don't you?"

"Who, Pele?"

"Mmm-hmm. Have you ever heard any stories of Pele?"

Paige stared down at her feet in the clear, cool water. "Aunt Naomi told me about Pele when I was a kid, but I don't remember much about the legend."

"In one myth, Pele can take the form of a beautiful woman," he said. He swirled sand underwater with his toe. "It's believed she appears to man when he's alone on the islands. Appears to a man and tempts him. And then…she disappears."

Paige looked over at him, mesmerized by the pensive look in his eyes. Was he thinking about her leaving? She had less than a week left at his club. And though she'd tried not to think about it, the thought of leaving made her feel empty. Alone.

Suddenly, she wanted Jack to pull her to him and kiss her, until that solemn look in his eyes faded to passion. Maybe it was time to finally share her heart for once in her life. The idea felt foreign to her, scary. But if she was going to do it, she knew right then and there that she wanted it to be with Jack.

She swallowed and took a step toward him. She tentatively reached her hand out to him. The waterfall echoed in the background, its stream bumping against their legs. She took Jack's hand and held it. Then she raised his fingers to her lips and kissed his palm. His light blue eyes darkened beneath her touch. She took a step closer, her feet squishing in the wet sand beneath the water. She slid her arms around his waist and moved her gaze along his sun-burnished hair, to his stubbled jaw, and down to the swell of his hard, muscled chest beneath his shirt. She let a smile of encouragement play across her mouth.

"Don't you want to kiss me, Jack?" she whispered.

CHAPTER TEN

JACK gazed down at the smiling invitation on Paige's lips. Hell, yes, he wanted to kiss her. This was what he'd been waiting for ever since she'd arrived at his resort, wasn't it?

Just like the myth of Pele, Paige had reappeared in his life and tempted him. But what came after that? In the legend, she disappeared. Jack swallowed. Would that happen with them, too? Would she leave on her departure date, never to be seen again?

In the beginning, his plan had been fun and games— a stolen kiss, innocent flirting—leaving her with a different image from the old Jack she used to know.

But where was the satisfaction of leaving her wanting, if it killed him to have her leave at all?

Damn it. He'd gotten caught up in his feelings for her all over again, and that definitely wasn't on his list.

She tightened her arms around his waist, and he saw his payback plan crumbling all around him. He gazed down at the warm, shy desire that shone in her eyes. He wanted this woman more than any woman he'd ever known.

She tickled her fingers along his spine, and he dragged in a quick breath. Hell, he couldn't focus when she touched him like that. Possessed by need, he decided he could sort his feelings out later. Right now, all he could focus on was the warm, soft woman in his arms, asking for his kiss.

He gave in to the urge and drew her closer. He lowered his head and kissed her upturned mouth, swallowing her tiny murmur of delight.

Her lips softened beneath his touch. He deepened the kiss, moving his hands from her waist, to her spine and down to her backside. *Paige.* His senses sprang to life, and the low, dull pull of desire gathered within him. He cupped the fleshy curve of her bottom and pressed her hips against him until his swelling jut of arousal made contact with the soft juncture of her thighs. He heard her sharp intake at the joining and kissed her deeper.

"Mmm, Jack." Her sexy whisper floated into the humid air, and the last of his control followed with it.

He bent down and placed his arm beneath her knees, sweeping her up and carrying her to the sand. In two quick strides, he'd laid her on the cool earth and covered the length of her body with his. He stared down at her, her green eyes passionate, a tempting little smile on her lips. He wanted to touch her, all of her.

She relaxed beneath him and ran a gentle hand along his cheek. It was a quiet touch. A touch that spoke of caring and hinted at promise.

His heart gave an exhilarating lurch in his chest. How far was this going to go? He'd initially meant the afternoon to end with a kiss, maybe a little more. But now…

Paige stared up at him, her eyes offering a silent invitation.

Without further thought, Jack reached for the buttons of her shirt. His hands trembled with need, and he bit back a quiet oath, thinking only of what was yet to come.

Paige gazed back at Jack and basked in the eager male arousal on his face. To think that she could bring him to that state pleased her beyond belief. She studied him as he focused on the buttons of her blouse. His attention on the task brought interesting lines of concentration to his face, adding to his attractive features. A hint of stubble darkened his jaw, and a wayward lock of hair fell across his forehead. His hungry hands made quick business of her last two buttons, and she sucked in a breath when his fingers swept across her bare skin.

He slid a finger beneath the front clasp of her bra, and with one flick he'd bared her. "Paige," he whispered with an almost imperceptible shake of his head. He slipped the last stitch of clothing from her shoulders and tossed it aside on the sand. When he returned his gaze to her, his smoldering look communicated his intent. He slid his hand over her and cupped her breast. He teased the tip between his fingers, then raised his gaze to her face. Slowly he lowered his head and captured her lips with a soft, searching kiss.

She returned his kiss, enjoying his rugged, masculine feel.

He trailed kisses along her throat, then moved lower to her breast. Gently, he drew her nipple into his mouth, teasing, coaxing until she arched beneath him with pleasure. She raked her fingers through his silky hair, and he moved to her other breast to claim it, as well.

He rose on one elbow and gazed down at her, his breathing rapid. In one swift motion, he tugged his shirt over his head, baring his tanned, muscular chest.

Paige sucked in a breath, taking in the swell of his pectorals that bunched and flexed with his movement. Daunting male power lay quiet beneath his skin.

He lowered himself until his chest lightly rested against hers. Her breasts softened beneath him, her nipples grazing his solid muscle. He breathed in softly. "You okay?" he asked, his voice husky.

She nodded.

He kissed her gently, and she savored his mouth. When she felt his tongue, she welcomed him inside. He kissed her long and deep until she lost all sense of time, aware only of the low whir of the waterfall...the cool, misty air against her flesh...and Jack's body above her.

His kisses turned hot and increasingly urgent. But when he reached for the zipper of her shorts, she tensed. He raised his head and looked down at her. His eyes glittered, heated and ready. "Decide now," he warned her softly, "because in a minute, there will be no turning back."

The low warning floated on the misty air around them, taunting her, tempting her.

"It *is* broad daylight," she said, feeling a sudden modesty. "And...and we're outside."

Jack grinned with pure male satisfaction. "Yep. We sure are."

"Wh…what about protection?"

He reached into the pocket of his shorts and pulled out his wallet.

"You always carry condoms in your wallet?" She eyed him with a teasing grin. "That's pretty presumptuous."

"Presumptuous?" He had the courtesy to look chagrined. "It's an old habit from school. Every guy carries a condom in his wallet. To be cool."

"Is that so? How many condoms did you go through back then?"

He glanced skyward, as if pretending to count in his head. "Uh…zero."

Her lips curved into a smile, and he lowered his head, kissing her, effectively halting all further discussion. When he rose up again, the hungry look in his gaze excited her.

"So, is that a yes?" he asked softly.

She nodded slowly.

At her consent, he groaned and crushed his lips to hers. His knuckles grazed the flesh below her navel as his fingers traveled lower, bringing her shorts down with him. When his hand reached her lace panties, he paused and glanced at the silky lingerie. "Aw, Paige, what are you trying to do to me?" He looked at her with a helpless grin. "You're killing me here." Her soft chuckle ended on a gasp when he stripped that last piece of lace from her body in one deft maneuver. In even less time, he rid himself of the rest of his clothes and was pressing his lean, warm—and very nude—frame against hers once again.

Paige trembled inside, her senses heightened and aware. Her knowledge was limited in this department, whereas Jack… She swallowed.

Judging by the confidence in his movement and ease with how he touched her, he knew what he was doing.

She felt inadequate and awkward—

He interrupted her thoughts with a kiss—soft, slow and sweet. And beneath that tender touch, all worry spiraled from her mind to disappear into the waterfall's swirling haze.

Jack honestly hadn't meant for the afternoon to end quite like this, but he planned to savor every second, every touch. He couldn't believe his good fortune to have Paige back in his life, nor could he believe how strongly he'd come to feel for her. He raised his head and gazed down at the woman in his arms.

Paige.

His eyes traveled over all that she was. Her midnight-black hair splayed across her sun-kissed shoulders and curved around her creamy, rose-tipped breasts. He lowered his head and placed a soft kiss on one puckered tip and felt it tighten further beneath his lips.

She wanted him. He knew by the look in her eyes and in the way that she kissed him, her body arching against him. The heady knowledge almost sent him over the edge. He breathed in her flowery scent that reminded him of sunshine and the island's springs. Jack relished the feel of her breasts in his hands. She moaned softly beneath his touch, and he knew he couldn't hold off much longer. He moved his thigh between her knees, and she parted her legs for him. He almost groaned with anticipation as he settled above her. *Paige.* Her name whispered through his mind. He was ready for her. Too ready. He was harder than hell, but he wanted to make this moment last.

She raised thick lashes, gazing up at him, a clever little smile on her lips. She ran her hands along his spine and lower to his backside.

A low groan rose in his throat, and in that moment Jack gave in to the urge and pushed forward with a careful thrust.

Her eyes widened for an instant, and then she held him closer.

He eased into her warmth. Once he was fully within her, he waited, savoring the feeling, the excruciating arousal. He slowly withdrew and pushed into her again, his knees pressing into the cool sand. "God, Paige," he whispered. He moved above her carefully and changed the angle, enjoying the feel and taking it slow.

The brown flecks in her earthy green eyes swirled like fallen leaves in an island stream. She uttered his name softly.

The hidden, tree-lined alcove provided a perfect shelter with its misty tropical foliage and high-reaching trees. Secluded, intimate—perfect for a lovers' tryst. Jack marveled at the afternoon's unexpected turn, their bodies entwined upon the cool earth, the light tones of their nude flesh a contrast against the wet, darkened sand beneath them. It was a heady, carnal feeling to couple in broad daylight, naked, natural, a breath away from scandal but, oh, so good. He enjoyed each thrust as much as the last, his movements as lazy as the river that swirled by.

Paige looped her arms around his neck and breathed his name against his throat.

Hearing his name on her lips warmed him, enticed him. A sudden rush of emotion swept over him. Feelings for her that surprised him by the sheer intensity.

The splash and chuckle of the waterfall filled the air around them.

"Jack." She moaned softly, shifting beneath him.

He increased his pace, and she rocked with him gently. He squeezed his eyes shut. If she kept that up, he was going to lose control. He lost himself inside her whispers, each flex of his muscles a rhythmic push toward satisfaction.

She moved her hands to his backside and pressed her fingers into his flesh, urging him to her.

Unable to help himself, he gave a harder thrust. Then another. Damn it, it felt too good. He grasped her hips to try to slow down, but his body betrayed him. Paige wrapped her legs around him, and Jack gave up all semblance of control and just let go, working himself into her with wild, frantic abandon.

She fisted her hands in the wet loose sand and cried his name once, twice…

Oh, God. "Paige." He lifted her hips, giving one final thrust toward exquisite release.

In the seconds that followed, Jack fought to reclaim

his breath, resting his forehead against hers. He stilled above her and buried his face in her silky black hair. The playful spatter of the waterfall sounded oddly like applause, and a small, satisfied smile curved his mouth. He breathed in deeply and wrapped his arms around the sexy, vibrant woman beneath him.

Slowly, Jack's smile faded. He'd been right when he'd said there would be no turning back. Because in that moment his harmless payback plan had turned into something far more serious.

Jack closed his eyes and sighed. He needed to take a step back, analyze his feelings for once in his life. The problem was, those feelings scared the hell out of him, and he wasn't sure he was ready to face them.

Paige rode the elevator downstairs from her room and entered Club Lealea's lobby. Making love with Jack the day before had been exhilarating, freeing. She'd never known sex could be so good. And their skinny-dip afterward? She grinned the same grin she'd been grinning ever since their tryst at the waterfall. My, oh, my. Her ridiculous grin deepened.

Yep, life was good. She'd come to love Club Lealea. And she was enjoying Hawaii. She'd forgotten the beauty of the islands, the laid-back attitude, the welcoming nature of the people who lived here. Maybe it was time to take charge of her life, make a change and return to Kauai...permanently. Because the thought of leaving the island, *and Jack*, was something she wasn't sure she could bring herself to do.

Besides, the opportunities for work and research were immeasurable here. She found the history of the islands and Polynesian culture fascinating. Heck, she'd been studying anthropology and ancient civilizations at university for years. It was one of her many varied interests. And with her passion for birds and plants…the options were endless.

Her vacation was almost over. And, frankly, she wanted more—more time in Hawaii and more time with the man she had come to love.

She shook her head, surprised at what her stint at the singles' club had done for her. Aunt Naomi had been right to send her here. Lately, Paige had felt wanton, confident and free. And dare she admit it…a little sexy.

She rounded the corner and scanned the area for Jack. She hadn't seen him since their "encounter", and, to tell the truth, she couldn't wait to see him again.

She crossed the lobby and found Aunt Naomi and Irene sitting at a round table with a group of young men. Paige squinted at them. What were they doing? Playing cards? She neared the table and looked closer.

Aunt Naomi glanced up and took the cigar out of her mouth. "Hey, Paige. Grab a chair and join us." She tugged at the baseball cap perched atop her frizzy orange curls and grinned.

"What are you playing?"

"Poker. Five Card Draw. You in?"

"No, thanks. I'll watch."

Naomi shrugged. "Suit yourself." She shuffled the cards.

One of the young guys at the table rubbed his hands together. "Okay, Naomi, it's your deal. Gimme some good ones this time. Daddy needs a new pair of shoes." He winked at her.

Paige stood and watched the game, glancing around the group. The guys at the club had taken a real shine to her aunt. She'd involved them in a Ping-Pong tournament, and now this. She was having a ball. Oh, and there was Kurt, sitting across the table with a fistful of cards in his hand.

He nodded to her and grinned.

And there was Handsome Boy from the pool.

Paige watched as the group continued to play. After a few rounds, her gaze wandered until, suddenly, Jack entered the lobby.

Her heart made an erratic leap, and she straightened.

His eyes met hers from across the room, and he smiled. She watched him make his way over.

Before Paige could say a word, Aunt Naomi spotted him. "Hiya, Jack," she said, her stogie clenched between her teeth. "Wanna play?"

"Ah, no. Thanks."

His easy gaze locked on Paige from across the table, and she instantly felt the change. It was an intimate feeling, a sense of closeness between them. He winked at her, and warmth expanded in her chest. She fought the impulse to rush to his side and, instead, played it cool and focused on the game.

Jack stood behind Irene's chair with his arms crossed.

"Your turn, Irene," Aunt Naomi said.

"Ha, finally." Irene grinned smugly. "Read 'em and weep, boys. I got a full house."

Jack glanced at Irene's cards and cleared his throat. He frowned pointedly at Naomi sitting to her right.

Naomi caught his look and leaned over to peek at Irene's cards. "No, hon. That's not a full house. But you do have a three of a kind, and that beats Kurt's two pairs, so you win the pot."

Irene chuckled with glee and reached her scrawny arms around the pile of chips in the middle of the table, scooting them to her side.

It was then that Paige noticed Irene's hair. It had reached staggering heights this afternoon. Paige bit her lip and shook her head. Apparently, what the old woman lacked in height, she'd decided to make up for with hair.

On the next go round, Irene exclaimed, "Oh, boy. I'm not sure what I have here, but I know it's good." She peered closer at the cards in her hand and thought for a moment. "Eh, what the heck? I'm all in." She shoved her entire pile of chips to the middle of the table.

"A-hem." Jack cleared his throat again from behind Irene and shook his head at Naomi.

Naomi leaned over and glanced at Irene's cards. "Irene, I don't see anything there."

"Huh? What do you call that? I bet it's a straight flush."

Aunt Naomi gave her a patient smile. "That's not a flush."

"Sure it is. They're all red."

"Yes, but they're not in sequence, and they aren't the same suit. See, that's a diamond, and that's a heart."

"Oh-h-h. Never mind." Irene dragged her chips out from the middle of the table. "I fold."

Just then, Lulu entered the lobby, and when she saw them she made her way over. Her floral Hawaiian sundress complemented her tan, and her long black hair swished against her shoulders.

"Hi, guys. What's going on?" she asked, smiling at the players. Her eyes cooled a bit as they landed on Paige.

"We're playing poker," Naomi said. "You in?"

Lulu wrinkled her pretty nose. "No, thanks. It's my day off. I just came in to see Jack."

"Oh, yeah?" Jack ran his hand through his sun-streaked hair. "What's up?"

"Well, I was hoping to speak with you privately."

"Oh. Uh, okay." He glanced at the others at the table. "You guys have fun." He tossed an apologetic look at Paige right as Lulu looped her arm through his. She pulled him outside to the pool.

Paige's heart sank. She watched through the windows as the two of them stood on the patio. Her old insecurities came crashing to the surface, and Paige felt a sudden uncertainty—feeling unsure about herself and her own appeal. Seeing Lulu with her hands on Jack, looking into his eyes and smiling, was enough to make her want to run out there and shove the activities coordinator into the pool, cute Hawaiian sundress and all.

Paige paused and took a moment to think. Surely Jack wasn't interested in Lulu at this point. Not after the waterfall. Not after the heated look in his eyes, the way he'd uttered her name on a low, throaty groan as he'd taken her over the edge. Surely, not after that. She needed to trust in herself.

But, unfortunately, it looked as if Lulu was still after Jack. Paige narrowed her eyes as she watched the young woman grasp Jack's hand, then put her palm on his chest as she spoke to him.

The more she watched the two of them, the more her determination grew. That was it. It was time to do something, because she'd be damned if she'd sit by and let Jack slip away. Today, she'd planned to take up with him where they'd left off, and that was exactly what she was going to do. It was time to seduce Jack once and for all.

Paige nodded slowly, her thoughts shifting to a woman's magazine Aunt Naomi had tossed in her suitcase. She'd read an article called, "Make Him Yours for Keeps." Perhaps it was time to study up on the subject. After all, book-learning was her forte, and she was a *very* good student. Maybe it was time for this good student to be a little naughty.

A slow smile crept across her lips. Yep, time to learn more about the art of seduction. Unbeknownst to him, Mr Jack Banta had an interesting night in store.

Her mental plan was interrupted by a chant going on at the poker table.

"Naomi—Naomi—Naomi." The raucous group of young guys was chanting her aunt's name as they waited for her to lay down her cards.

Aunt Naomi paused for dramatic effect, then laid down a three of a kind, all aces.

The guys groaned with good humor, and she won the pot.

Paige smiled. Leave it to Aunt Naomi to charm a table full of twenty-year-olds.

"Ah-h-h, it's good to win," Naomi said. "Now that I have all these chips, maybe it's time to raise the stakes. Anyone up for a round of strip poker?"

Several eyes widened, and a few chairs pushed back from the table. A chorus of voices muttered, "No, thanks… Gee, look at the time… Hoo-wee, I'm tired… 'Bout time for dinner."

A voice chirped up from off to the side. "Sounds good to me!"

All eyes turned to an old janitor who'd been pushing a mop nearby. A mischievous grin played across his wrinkled face.

Aunt Naomi's eyes perked up.

Paige groaned. "Oh, no. I'm outta here." She followed on the heels of the rest of the table, leaving Naomi, Irene and their new friend to do what they liked.

Jack shoved his paperwork to the side and scrubbed his hands over his face. He leaned back in his office chair and checked his watch. Ten-thirty. It was late.

He wondered what Paige was doing right now. He hadn't seen her since Lulu had dragged him away from the poker game this afternoon. He clenched his teeth at the reminder.

Lulu must have sensed what was going on between

him and Paige, because she'd pulled him from the card game in a last-ditch effort to tempt him.

Jack sighed. He'd been forced to sit down with her and make it clear that he wasn't interested, and that, in any case, since he was her boss, it would be inappropriate. He supposed he should've nipped it in the bud sooner, but he'd been hoping she'd just let it go.

He rubbed his hand along the back of his neck. Lulu was a good employee. He hoped they could put it behind them and continue forward from here. As for Paige...

He chewed the inside of his lip and picked a pen up off his desk, toying with it. Talk about mind-blowing sex. Their experience at the waterfall had been the best sex of his entire life. Of course, the fact that it had been with Paige had been a large part of why it had been so good. Jack sighed. Truth be told, she was the reason he was sitting in his office at ten-thirty on a work night, hiding out. Actually, he wasn't hiding, *per se,* but he also wasn't ready to face his feelings for her. And it didn't help that her checkout date was approaching. There wasn't much time.

When push came to shove, he had to agree that she'd been right about him all along. He was afraid of rejection. Afraid she would reject him in the end, just as she had back in school, just as everyone else had left him in his life. And, damn it, he wasn't sure he was up for another rejection, should things go wrong. Not at this stage in the game. Back in school, he'd been a kid, with youthful, immature emotions. But this time around, they were adults, and the depth of what he felt was on a much grander scale.

He sighed and recentered the piece of paper he'd

been working on in front of him. It was another list. A list of work goals he'd been going over. Number One: Prepare business plan for the upcoming year. *Check.* He'd just finished that this week. Number Two: Interview new hula dancer for Lealea Luau. *Check.*

He doodled on the margin, making a swirl at the end of his checkmark. God, he loved marking things off his lists. It felt good. Productive. And it helped take his mind off his situation with Paige.

He read Number Three. Call new accountant that had been recommended to him. *Check.* He made an exaggerated flourish, liking the bold slash he'd just made.

"Still making lists these days, I take it?" A feminine voice broke the silence from the doorway.

Startled, he glanced up to find Paige at the entry.

Jack did a double take and dropped his pen.

She wore a simple black dress, sleek in its lines, with narrow straps showing off the slender shape of her bare arms—the same warm, smooth bare arms that had clung to him beneath the waterfall after their tryst. Remembrances flickered through his mind of their wet lips, fervent, kissing, while the splash of the falls streamed over their nude bodies.

He stared back at her, and his mouth went dry. The black fabric hugged her curves with a simple, casual elegance, her breasts offering the perfect hint of cleavage. Not in your face, not flashy. Just…Paige.

"You, uh—" he coughed "—you look nice. Going somewhere?"

"No. I just went out to dinner with Aunt Naomi and

Irene. I called your suite to see if you'd like to join us, but I couldn't find you."

"Oh. I was working."

"I see that." She smiled softly and closed the door behind her. "Another one of Jackson Banta's famous lists?"

He felt himself redden beneath her playful smile.

She stepped closer to his desk, her delicate black sandals clicking against the hardwood floor. "Anything I can help you—" she lowered her voice to a seductive level "—cross off?"

Jack was having a hard time focusing on her words, not to mention forming his own. She was distracting. And so was that sexy whiff of perfume that tickled his nose and enticed him. What had she asked? If she could help him with his list? He swiveled in his chair. *She's just hit a little too close to home for comfort.*

She toyed with a black pen that stood upright in a holder on his desk.

He watched her provocative fingers slowly stroke up and down.

"I know it's late," she said, "but I was wondering if you could pencil me in on your list of things…*to do*."

Jack made a peculiar choking sound and covered it by clearing his throat. *If only she knew.*

She helped herself, sitting on the edge of his desk, an everyday move that, when done by her, in that dress, seemed sexier than anything he thought he'd ever seen.

"Sure, I can, er, pencil you in," he said. "I was just about finished here." He reached for the list he'd been working on and gave a little tug. She was sitting on the edge of his paper.

"Oh, sorry." She lifted her hip, moving her curvaceous, tempting rear-end off his list. "Perhaps I should sit somewhere else?" She studied him, a clever look in her eyes, then walked around the desk to his side.

He cocked his head. What was she doing? She drew closer, and he shifted in his seat. "What, um, what's going on?"

"Oh, nothing. I'm just having a seat. The best seat in the house." She swiveled his chair toward her, jerking him along with it, and before he knew it she'd straddled him.

Good Lord. Jack stared at the woman on his lap. Her dress hitched high on her thighs, a hint of black lace panties peeking out.

What was happening here?

She laced her fingers through his hair.

He smothered a groan and closed his eyes. That felt good. He leaned his head back. She didn't have to do this. Couldn't she tell he was crazy about her already? Paige was the only woman he wanted. The only woman he'd ever wanted.

That thought halted the slow smile that had tipped up the corners of his mouth. What was he doing? The more time he spent with her, the deeper he'd get and the harder he'd fall in the end.

He opened his eyes and looked up at her. This was not the same woman he'd known back in school. Heck, this wasn't the same woman who'd walked through his door a couple of weeks ago. This new woman was unrestrained, and there was a spark of sexual curiosity in her gaze.

He felt a twinge of arousal low in his stomach, clouding his judgement. He became highly aware of the warm, gentle curves that wriggled in his lap.

Hell. He didn't want to think about the future, didn't want to think about his feelings, or what would happen tomorrow. All he wanted to do was enjoy whatever was going on here. Now. On his lap.

She pursed her lips into what she probably thought was a sexy look.

It was.

Amused by her seduction and more than a little aroused, Jack eased back in his chair and decided to see how far she was willing to go…

CHAPTER ELEVEN

OH, YES. She was going all the way. Paige gazed down at the man beneath her. At seventeen, he'd been serious, shy. But, dear God, all grown up, he was breathtaking.

Jack looked good behind a businessman power-desk. As if he belonged there, making decisions and giving orders. And suddenly Paige was aware of the years that had passed since they'd last seen each other.

It gave her a sense of empowerment to take charge of the situation. Go after what she wanted. Entice him. Seduce him. Make him hers. And by the smoldering look in his eyes, that was exactly what she was doing.

"The work day is over," she said, letting her voice drop to a husky level. She unbuttoned the top of his light blue Lealea shirt. "Time for play, don't you think?"

He lowered his gaze to her fingers as she released each button, one by one. "Sure."

She watched him gulp and grinned to herself. She had planned to lure him to her room, but seeing him behind his desk in his work clothes had made her want to rumple him a bit. Heck, a tumble on his desk might be fun. She was going all out tonight, forcing herself from her comfort zone. So why not?

"You don't need this tee shirt underneath either, do you?" she asked, tugging it over his head. His collar dragged across his hair, leaving it in sexy disarray. "Mmm…that's better." She ran her hands over his bare chest, and his pectoral muscles tensed beneath her palms.

When she reached between her legs for the buckle of his belt, she felt his quick intake of breath. She arched an eyebrow. "Shall I stop?"

He flicked his tongue over his lips. "No," he croaked. "You're, ah, you're doing fine."

She tugged at his buckle and released it, pleased to find the erection beneath his zipper. Emboldened by the clear evidence of his desire for her, she lowered his zipper, inch by inch, then looped her fingers inside the waistband of his boxers. His abdomen tightened beneath her fingers, as she grazed his flesh.

He sucked in a breath and closed his eyes.

She enjoyed the intimacy of encircling his smooth skin, knowing she was touching the most innervated spot on his body. He clenched one fist as if restraining himself against the intensity, his other hand grasping the arm of the chair.

Soon, he reached down and stilled her hand. "You might want to slow down a bit," he warned, his voice hoarse with need. "Besides, you're overdressed for our little office party, don't you think?"

Before she knew it, he reached behind her and grasped the zipper of her dress. He zipped it all the way down, the sound announcing his intent into the silence of the room. Jack slowly slid the straps from her shoulders. He leaned forward and trailed his lips down her chest, following the fabric, until he'd lowered the dress to her waist.

Paige trembled with desire. Mmm, how she wanted this man. She'd never felt the need, the primal urge, to be with a man more than she did in that very moment. She rose from his lap and stood in front of him, allowing her dress to pool at her feet. She kicked her sandals off and stood before Jack in a pair of black lace panties and bra.

His eyes flickered, heated and wanting, as he moved his gaze slowly over the length of her body.

She dipped her finger into the cup of her bra and pulled out a condom with a sly grin.

Jack's eyebrows rose. "Now that's presumptuous if I've ever seen it."

"Every girl carries a condom in her bra—" she winked and repeated his earlier words "—to be cool."

With an appreciative smile, he took the condom and then released the clasp of her bra, freeing her breasts to his unwavering gaze. "God, Paige," he murmured. He leaned forward and ran his finger over her nipple. She felt it swell beneath his touch. Then he cupped her breast fully in his hand, letting it fill the curve of his palm before leaning forward and capturing the tip between his lips. Paige bit back a moan as his hands roamed over her sides then moved lower to squeeze her bottom. In one deft maneuver, he slipped her lacy black lingerie down her legs.

She waited as he drank in the sight of her, surprised

by her lack of modesty. At this point, she didn't care. She wanted Jack. That was all there was to it. Past the point of no return, and not allowing herself to think her way out of her plan, she reached forward and pushed his chest, shoving him back against his chair.

His eyes widened with surprise. Then, his lips hitched into a half smile.

She stepped forward to straddle him again, but he shook his head. "Uh-uh." He grabbed her by the waist and lifted her up, so that she didn't just straddle his legs, but she straddled the arms of the chair, as well.

She gasped, and he winked. "That's right." He cocked a grin. "I figure if we're going to do this, we might as well do it right." With that, he shifted beneath her, and she felt the tip of his arousal at the splayed juncture of her thighs.

Oh, my. Paige swallowed and realized there was nothing left to do but— She lowered herself down along his hardened length. *Oh, my.* She closed her eyes and eased further.

Jack leaned his head back against the chair and groaned softly.

She raised up, teased him for a moment, and lowered again.

His eyes darkened.

She began a slow rhythm, taking charge and moving at will. She liked the contrast of her nude flesh against the staid formality of his office. It added to her sense of indiscretion—having sex in his workplace. Naughty, but, oh, so satisfying.

Jack grabbed her waist, his fingers gently digging into her flesh. "God, Paige, you don't know what you're doing to me." His breath hissed between his teeth, and he thrust his hips up to meet her.

She grinned to herself, knowing exactly what she was doing, thanks to the articles she'd read. It was a powerful feeling, bringing Jack to the brink of losing control.

Jack lost himself in her every rise and fall, each movement a warm, gentle parting toward satisfaction. Mmm, what this woman did to him. If she had been any other woman, he might have had more control. But with this particular woman? He was lost.

He grasped her hips to guide her along his swollen length and swallowed her resulting murmur of assent.

What he really needed was more room to do this properly. Taking matters into his own hands, he leaned forward and swept folders and papers off his desk with one arm.

Paige gasped, while falling pens and notebooks clattered to the floor.

Surprise switched to understanding along her features, and she hopped up onto his desk. She relaxed back with a welcoming smile, and Jack smothered a groan of approval.

He knew that this image of her would remain imprinted in his mind for ever. All he could see was the woman he had come to know. The woman he had grown to feel more strongly for than anyone in his entire life. She looked beautiful in that moment. Her hair tousled, an inviting smile on her mouth, the curve and sway of her breasts a gentle summons.

Jack made room for himself between her soft, silky thighs. One of these days, he was going to have her on a bed and do things right.

In the moments that followed, sounds of pleasure slipped from her throat, enticing him, exciting him, compelling him onward. He moved inside her, taking his time, and savoring the feel, but soon he felt himself losing control. He mumbled something incoherent in a state of ecstasy and worked his way into her with more purpose.

"Oh, Jack." She clutched the edge of his desk, her voice undeniably excited.

A satisfied smile curved Jack's lips, and that was when he came undone. He gave several final, urgent thrusts, and together they spiraled over the edge, a tangle of limbs and sated murmurs.

The next afternoon, after a late lunch and some shopping, Paige strolled through the Lealea lobby, indulging in the free and easy beat of her heart. The night before had put a smile on her face and a skip to her step that she hadn't felt since…well, since for ever.

The new floral sundress she'd just purchased swished gaily about her legs as she made her way to the pool. She rarely wore dresses, but she'd acted on impulse, buying it with Jack in mind. Lately she'd been more spontaneous, loosening her rigid structure and trying new things. She blushed at the thought of making love with Jack in his office the night before.

Trying new things, indeed.

Paige smiled softly to herself and enjoyed the delicate fragrance of the flowers that lined the concrete pathway. Humming out loud, she entered the sun-splashed patio.

"Boy, someone seems happy today."

She paused to find Lulu following her into the pool area with a stack of white beach towels under her arm.

"Hi, Lulu." She smiled at the young woman, her newfound confidence restored after her night with Jack.

"What are you so happy about?" Lulu asked, her tone casual.

"Hmm? Oh, I don't know. Just happy to be here, I guess."

The coordinator's eyes narrowed slightly, and she shook her head. "I'm not buying it. Only a man can put a smile on a woman's face like that. And I'm willing to bet that man's name is Jack." She gave her a knowing wink.

"Mmm, maybe." Paige wasn't entirely comfortable discussing Jack with Lulu, of all people. What was she up to now?

Lulu shaded her brow from the sun. "You know, when you first got here, I was sure you and Jack were rivals. I'm surprised how things have turned out."

"Really? Why did you think we were rivals?"

Lulu shrugged a tan, delicate shoulder. "I heard Jack mutter something about a payback when you first walked into the club." She studied Paige intently. "Guess it's none of my business. I just found it curious and have wondered what the payback was. But you two seem to be hitting it off well enough."

Paige frowned. "That's odd. I wonder what he meant about paybacks."

"I don't know." Lulu shrugged again, and a sly little smile curved the edges of her mouth. "Well, never mind. You seem pretty happy, so, whatever the payback was, you must've liked it."

The bell rang out at the towel hut, and Lulu glanced over with a sigh. "More people needing more towels. The hut just ran out." She adjusted the stack of towels under her arm. "I've got to go. See you later." With that, she strode away.

Paige remained where she stood, in the middle of the concrete pathway, her thoughts mixing inside her head. Payback? What was Lulu talking about? Had Jack planned some kind of payback for her?

A speculation formed in the back of her mind, and she frowned. Had he decided to pay her back for rejecting him years ago? She thought back to how baffled she'd been when Jack had kept popping up at her side when she'd first arrived at his club. Had it all been part of a plan to sleep with the girl who once got away? And then what? Drop her?

Surely that wasn't the case. He wouldn't do something like that. Would he? Seduce her into sleeping with him, just to get even with her for something? Without any true feelings involved? Surely he cared for her as she did him.

Or did he?

Questions careened through Paige's mind, and she wondered if Lulu was just trying to get inside her head.

Because it sickened her to even have such thoughts about a man she'd come to love.

Hating herself for doubting him this way, Paige turned on her heel to find Jack.

Paige found Jack in his office.

His face broke into a soft smile when he saw her. "Hey, you." He pushed his paperwork to the side. "Come on in."

Seeing him again, after the night they'd shared, made her heart stand still for a second. She watched him toy with a pen in his hands, remembering how those fingers had felt the night before, warm and slightly rough, as they'd moved along her body.

His easy gaze wandered over her, deliberate, appreciative. "Wow, a dress last night and another one today?" He paused. "You look good. I like it."

Just that sexy shift in his tone. That was all it took to make her heart take a crazy swerve.

"Have a seat," he offered.

She walked to the chair in front of his desk and stood behind it, rather than sitting.

"What?" Jack said. "You don't want the best seat in the house, this time?" He glanced down at his lap, then wriggled his eyebrows, a good-natured smile on his face.

He gazed back at her, and the laughter faded from his eyes. He tilted his head. "What's up?" He leaned forward and rested his elbows on the desk—the very desk that had felt smooth and cool beneath her back as he'd driven her out of her mind with pleasure.

"Are you busy?" Paige swallowed. "I was wondering if I could talk to you."

"I'm never too busy for *you*."

His smooth voice drifted over her, and she hated what she was about to ask. Paige drew in a slow breath. "Listen, um, I just spoke with Lulu by the pool, and she…" She paused, not sure how to say it. She felt like an idiot. But she needed to know. "Lulu said something about a payback. Do you know what she's talking about? She heard you say it was payback time when I first walked into the club."

Jack moved his elbows off the desk and leaned back in his chair. "A payback? I…ah…" He coughed. "A payback plan, you say?" He swiveled in his chair and rubbed the back of his neck.

Why wasn't he saying something? Anything. "Jack, you didn't try to seduce me as some sort of payback for not going out with you in school, did you?"

A hint of guilt adjusted itself quietly across his features.

Paige's heart sank, straight to the hardwood floor. She shook her head slowly. So, he didn't really have true feelings for her?

He'd never told her he loved her. He'd never even said he cared. She'd just assumed he felt the same way she did.

Her old insecurities came flooding back in a rush. Suddenly, she felt like the little girl who'd been dropped off by her busy parents at Naomi's house, yet again. Feeling unwanted, unloved. With nowhere else to go. She glanced down at her fingers that clutched the back of the chair. Her knuckles were white. She released her grip.

Paige steeled herself. "So, you don't really care about me? What did you do, Jack? Come up with one of your little lists? Write down ways to pay back Paige Pipkin, the girl who once turned you down?"

Jack paled, and his eyes darted away from her.

"Oh. My. God. You did!" Outraged, she stared back at him in disbelief. "Did you get a thrill out of crossing me off? I can just see it. Hike with Paige." She made a mark with her finger in the air. "*Check.* Dinner with Paige. *Check.* Kiss Paige—" Her voice broke. "*Check.*"

Gathering her anger, she smacked the palms of her hands on his desk and leaned in. "What else was on the list? Seduce Paige? Sleep with Paige? Check and *check?*" Her last check hit a shrill note, ringing out into the tense silence of his office. She drew in a shuddering breath and pushed off his desk.

Jack shifted in his chair, a sick look on his face. "Listen, Paige." His voice was hoarse. He cleared his throat. "Originally, I may have been thinking about payback, but—"

"Excuse me, Jack." Someone interrupted him from the open doorway.

Paige turned.

A Club Lealea employee stood in the entry. "Uh, we have a problem," he said. "We have a group of ten who just showed up, but we don't have them in our records. They've got reservation numbers, but they're not matching what I have in the books, and we're full. I don't have rooms for them."

Jack sighed and raked his fingers through his hair. "Have Nick handle it. I'm busy here."

The employee shook his head. "I would, but the fire alarm went off in the east wing. A false alarm. It's driving everyone crazy, and Nick's over there trying to shut it off."

"Did you notify the fire department that it's a false alarm?" Jack asked.

The muffled wail of fire sirens and tires screeching up curbside answered his question.

The employee grimaced. "Guess no one thought to call the fire department."

A muscle twitched along Jack's jaw. "Paige, I—"

She held up her hand. She'd heard enough from him. He'd already admitted the reason he'd seduced her. She'd been a fool to assume he cared for her, when he'd never told her how he really felt. What had she been thinking?

She backed away from his desk, her eyes blurring with unshed tears. She turned and pushed past his employee in the doorway.

"Paige, wait!"

Shaking her head, she rushed out, unable to look at him any longer.

God, she'd been a fool.

Paige stuffed clothing into her suitcase, her hands trembling. She couldn't stay here any longer. She wasn't due to check out yet, but she didn't care. She'd pay whatever it cost to change her plane tickets.

She clenched her teeth and tossed her hairbrush and

a magazine into her bag. She paused and stared at the magazine cover. "Ten Ways to Better Orgasms." *Yeah, right.* She pursed her lips. She'd found a better orgasm, all right. But it had been attached to a stupid payback plan. She took the magazine out of her suitcase and chucked it across the room into the trashcan. Cramming a pair of socks into some shoes, she slammed them into her suitcase.

Damn him.

She lifted a tee shirt off the bed and uncovered the pocket-sized birdcall book Jack had given to her. She picked it up and shook her head. Nothing but a reminder of his betrayal. She hated to throw away a book. It seemed like sacrilege. But to hell with him, she thought indignantly. And to every other tool of seduction he'd used to tempt her. A sob caught in her throat. Blinded by tears, she flung the book toward the trash—hard. It smacked against the wall and slid down, thudding against the rim of the can and missing its mark. It landed with a soft splutter of pages against the carpet.

Paige swiped the back of her hand across her cheeks, drying her face.

The bird book mocked her from its spot on the floor.

She scowled at it.

She peered closer and saw that it had fallen open to a section titled "Male Courtship—A Call for Every Purpose."

She narrowed her eyes. Apparently, Jack only had one call in his repertoire. And love had nothing to do with it.

She shook her head. And to think he'd been able to

maneuver *her* into making the first move. There ought to be a section in the book for warning calls. "When Good Birds Go Bad."

Paige sank onto the bed. She'd been considering a future with Jack. She'd thought about a life with him, maybe giving up her studies and moving back to Hawaii. And somewhere, in a tiny corner of her heart, she'd hoped that he loved her as she loved him. Maybe enough to contemplate something more serious, something permanent…like marriage. Fresh tears threatened, and she bit them back fiercely. How could she have been so wrong about him? She was a smart woman. She should've put two and two together—the invitation to his suite, the little gifts, the kisses… All a careful crafting to seduce her, make her care for him…and get even with her.

Now, she faced returning to California. Alone. Back to her old life. Back to her studies. Back to living with Aunt Naomi.

Suddenly, her old life looked bleak. Unfulfilling, tedious. She'd never known how lonely she'd been until she'd had a taste of a different way. Her stay at Lealea had opened her eyes to fun, excitement, a life outside the university.

Paige swiped at a runaway tear and rose to gather her toiletries from the bathroom. She'd have to find Naomi and let her know she was leaving. *Leaving.* The very idea brought a sad, dull feeling to her stomach. She wanted to cry—cry for the disappointed, broken remains of her heart that huddled in her chest.

She stepped onto the balcony and stared down at the

pool below. The late-afternoon winds brushed through her hair, shifting it across her shoulders and lifting loose tendrils upon the breeze. She'd grown to love this resort with its pool, the palm trees, the fun activities, the people. She'd been having the time of her life. But, most of all, being with Jack had brought her joy. She'd reveled in the budding of new love. The excitement that fluttered in her chest upon seeing him. And, more than anything, she'd come to have hope for a new future. *With Jack.*

But all of that had been dashed to bits in the matter of a heartbeat.

Would she ever find true love? Maybe she was destined to live life alone.

She let out a long, slow breath.

The sweet smell of tropical flowers floated on the breeze, but at the moment their pungent fragrance made her feel ill. Brooding thoughts swirled through her mind, and she stared down at the bustling poolside patio, unseeing. Eventually, the soft beat of drums drifted across the balcony along with the sounds of musicians taking to the stage. The early evening luau must be gearing up to begin soon. The discordant warm-up twangs of a ukulele echoed through a microphone somewhere near the beach.

Paige had come to enjoy the evening luaus. She smiled softly through her sorrow and leaned against the deck rail. She was different than the woman who had dreaded her first luau at the resort. She'd grown used to meeting new people.

She stared down at the pool. Singles were slowly rising

from their beach chairs and stretching, gathering their towels and straw hats to get ready for the luau.

She sighed. She might be leaving Club Lealea, but, when she really thought about it, she was actually returning home as a new woman. She nodded to herself, her mind slowly working its way out of its cloud of despondence.

It was time to move out of her aunt's house when she got back. She should leave the nest, forge a path of her own. Her thoughts drifted through her mind, slowly gathering speed. That was right. She could get a real job. Take life as it came, rather than hide behind her books.

The decision gave her hope.

Jack might have broken her heart, but she could pick up and move forward on her own.

Holding onto that thought as tightly as she could, she turned from the balcony and ducked back inside. Adding the last of her clothes to her bag, she banged her suitcase shut.

It was the sound of finality.

She clicked the old, rusty snaps closed, echoing her determination into the quiet of the room.

All that was left was to call the bellboy and then let Aunt Naomi know she was leaving.

She took one last look at the room that had been her private haven over the last few weeks. It had been welcoming and cheery with its tropical décor. Her lips curved into a rueful smile. She was definitely going to miss this place.

Paige took a deep breath and straightened her shoulders. It was time to face a new beginning.

* * *

Jack paced behind the reception desk in the lobby and glanced at his watch. Damn it, it was getting late. Where was Paige? The sun was going down, and she was nowhere to be found. After dealing with the fire department and the ten-person reservation mix-up, he'd called her room to no avail. He'd checked the pool, he'd gone up to her suite, and he'd been on the lookout for her in the lobby. But no Paige.

He picked up the phone at the front desk and dialed her room again. The low, dull sound of unanswered rings echoed through the receiver. Four rings. Five. *Come on, pick up the phone.* He tugged on the cord to allow more room to pace. Six rings. He stopped and tapped a pen on the marble countertop. Seven. Each ring added a measure of panic to his urgency. Eight.

He uttered an oath and banged the phone down. Jack scrubbed his hands through his hair. He was going to lose her. He stared down at the counter and felt desperation kick around inside his gut. A desperation like none he'd ever felt before. Losing Paige was going to cost him. Because, try as he might, he hadn't been able to curb his feelings for her. Now, his worst fears were coming true. If she left him, he was going to miss her more than he'd ever believed possible.

He glanced up to find Nick entering the reception area. "The fire department is still testing our alarm system," Nick said. "And it seems to have some problems. The fire chief wants to talk to you about maybe getting a new one."

Jack shook his head. Not now. He was about to lose Paige, and she was far more important than this.

He left the counter and clapped Nick on the shoulder as he walked past. "You handle it. I've got something to take care of."

"But…but I don't know what kind of system we should get."

Jack gave him a weary grin. "You're my assistant manager. I trust you to figure it out." With that, he left a surprised Nick to deal with the situation on his own.

A bellboy pushed a luggage cart out of the elevator and stopped beside the front desk. He lifted a suitcase off the cart and dropped it with a thud onto the marble floor.

Jack's heart dropped right along with it. *Paige's bag.*

The ridiculous daisy sticker smiled up at him from its spot on the worn-out suitcase.

He swallowed, shaken. Yep, Paige was leaving him. Somehow he had to stop her. If she wasn't in her room, then she must be somewhere on the grounds.

Jack strode through the lobby and checked the Tiki Lounge.

No Paige.

Maybe she'd gone to the luau for one last hurrah. Quickening his pace, he made his way outdoors. He walked down the concrete pathway at a good clip and followed the tiki torches that skirted the pool.

The sound of his purposeful stride cut through the muggy evening air, while the murmur of gathering voices drifted from the beachside luau. Jack made his way through the impending darkness into the pool area.

Suddenly, he stopped in his tracks.

Paige stood next to the shimmering blue of the underwater pool lights, talking with her aunt and Irene. As he entered the patio they ceased their discussion and looked over at him.

He stopped for a moment, and his heartbeat stalled in his chest.

Paige had her hand out in front of her in suspended conversation. Slowly, she dropped her hand to her side and stared back at him in silence.

He took a deep breath and continued toward them, wondering how badly Aunt Naomi wanted to kick his ass right about now.

He felt bad enough to do it for her, if he were more limber.

He approached their three-woman powwow with what he hoped was a penitent smile. "Evening, ladies." He turned to Paige and softened his voice. "I've been looking all over for you."

Her expression remained stoic, and she didn't respond.

Jack gulped and shifted his gaze to Naomi and Irene. Coconut bikini tops covered their wrinkled chests, and their festive grass skirts rustled cheerfully over their hips. But judging by the looks aimed his way, they were feeling anything but cheery toward him. Hell. Things didn't look promising.

"Going to the luau?" A completely inane question, but he asked it anyway.

"Uh-huh." Aunt Naomi looked him up and down, her arms crossed. She snorted and shook her head at him.

"Come on, Irene. I think these two need some time alone."

Irene scrunched her face into a jumble of wrinkled disdain. "I'm right behind you, Naomi." She snorted, too, and grabbed her four-pronged walking cane. As she stomped past Jack she plunked one prong firmly over the top of his foot for good measure.

"Hey!" He hopped backward on one foot. Frowning, Jack rubbed his toe. He straightened and glanced at Paige.

Her lips had twisted into a smirk—her first sign of emotion.

Jack figured any emotion was better than nothing. Encouraged, he said, "Paige, I didn't get a chance to explain something when you were in my office earlier."

She put her hand on her hip. "I got my answer. You admitted you seduced me into sleeping with you as a payback." She shrugged coolly. "Enough said."

Just then, a fire alarm sounded in the distance, coming from the west wing of the hotel this time.

"Look," Paige said. "You're busy. Go fix your alarm. I have a plane to catch." She turned to leave.

"No." He grasped her shoulders, his hands resting over the silky black hair that slipped across her warm skin. "I don't care about the alarm." He gazed down at her. Her hair was long and loose, the way he liked it. "Hell, the whole sprinkler system can go off in the lobby, for all I care. Right now, all that matters is you. Paige, I didn't plan to seduce you."

"You didn't?"

He shook his head. "No." He released her shoulders

and sighed. God, he hated confrontation. How had things come to this? "Listen, I may have come up with a stupid payback plan, but sleeping with you wasn't part of it."

"It wasn't?" She didn't look convinced.

"No."

"Then what was the plan?"

"Well, uh…" It had sounded much better in his head at the time. But when forced to explain it out loud, it sounded pretty lame. "Look, when I saw you walk into my club, I was shocked to see you. And in the spur of the moment, I suddenly remembered how…" He rubbed his jaw. This wasn't easy. He hated putting himself out there. He drew in a long breath. "I remembered how attracted I'd been to you back in school."

He paused and watched her. She didn't seem surprised by the revelation. But, then again, he'd asked her out so many times, it couldn't come as much of a surprise that he'd pined for her. That was what had spawned the whole payback plan in the first place.

"I'm sure you knew how I felt back then. And frankly—" he swallowed around his discomfort "—the rejection hurt." There. He'd said it. He sighed and continued. "So, when I saw you walk through my doors, I thought it might be satisfying to make you want me…the way I once wanted you. Give you a taste of what you passed up years ago. Make you feel the way you made me feel and then, drop you. Leave you wanting the guy you once snubbed. But, the first time I tried it, I started to care for you. And the more I was around you, the more I fell for you all over again." He cleared his throat and watched her take in his words. "Paige," he said softly. "In all honesty, sleeping with you wasn't part of the plan. I truly didn't mean for things to go quite that far."

He watched a mixture of emotions play across her face. She seemed initially surprised by his statement, followed by a consideration of the truthfulness of his words, a weighing of the evidence…and he knew the instant she came to her conclusion. She wasn't buying it. Not completely. Damn it. He understood why she might feel skeptical. But he'd told the truth. Typically, he appreciated her analytical mind. He always had. It was one of the many things he loved about her. But at the moment, her intelligence was working against him.

Wait a minute. Back up a step. What was that? *Her analytical mind was one of the many things he loved about her.* Why had it taken him so long to realize it?

He loved her.

Jack knew it in that instant. And somewhere in the recesses of his mind, he'd known it all along. He just hadn't wanted to admit it. Because acknowledging it would mean he could get hurt—when she rejected him in the end.

And wasn't that what was happening right now? She was going to leave. Just as he'd known she would. The same way she'd deserted the Jackson Banta of the past.

"I don't know, Jack," she said. "I find it hard to believe that you didn't plan to sleep with me." She chewed her bottom lip, a delicate wrinkle of doubt marring her forehead. "To be honest with you, I was excited when I found you at this club. We'd been such good friends in school. And the whole time I've been here, I've been looking for that sweet, intelligent guy I used to know." She squinted at him through the glittering blue-green light. "Is the guy I used to know still in there? I catch glimpses of him now and then." She studied him, her eyes traveling over his face.

Jack swallowed.

"Or are you the flashy resort owner?" she said. "The new guy, the one with the immature payback plan?" She gazed up at him. "Which is it, Jack?"

He stared back at Paige, her question hovering in the air between them. Hell, he was the same guy she used to know. Everything else was a façade. But did he dare share his heart with this woman yet again? Tell her he loved her? Let her know he was the same guy she rejected years ago?

Disappointment, disillusion, everything a man didn't want to see in the eyes of the woman he loved flickered through her gaze. He needed to act now, because he was about to lose her once and for all. It was time to add a fifth item to his list—Tell Paige he loved her.

Check.

No, he paused.

More like check*mate*.

He took a deep breath and readied himself to bare his soul and risk the most humiliating rejection of his life. In school, he'd been a kid with a boyhood crush. But now, for the first time ever, Jack Banta was in love.

And it scared the hell out of him.

CHAPTER TWELVE

PAIGE waited for Jack's answer. Was he just a playboy who'd seduced her? Had he seen her as an intriguing little diversion—to see if he could sleep with the girl who'd once gotten away? Or was he really the same guy she used to know—smart and kind and concerned for those around him? He'd said he hadn't aimed to get her in bed. Was that true?

"Paige," he said softly. "I admit that my payback was foolish. I didn't mean to hurt you, and I didn't mean for it to go that far. I'm telling you the truth."

Her heart remained prickly, coiled tight, not ready to relax for fear of being hurt. And it didn't help that his low, soft tone reminded her of the sensual voice that had murmured in her ear as they'd made love at the waterfall. The same voice that had gasped her name in a state of ecstasy in his office the night before.

He gave her a small, sad smile, and her heart, traitor that it was, let a piece of anger relax from its spiteful ball.

"And to answer your question—" he paused and ran his fingers through his dark blond hair "—I…I'm not the flashy resort-owner guy, Paige. I'm the same guy you knew in school. Just a little older and hopefully a little wiser. Although—" he gave her a guilty-looking grin "—although you might not have noticed the wise part." His mouth curved to the side in an embarrassed but adorable twist.

She so wanted to believe him.

"It's just that I didn't have much luck with the girls in school." He gave her a pointed look. Then his tone softened. "Especially with the one I really wanted." He shrugged and made a thin, hollow laugh. "Guess I was trying to make up for my past."

Paige could tell he was making light of things. But in that soul-baring moment, she finally saw the pain he'd worked so hard to hide. It was in the rasp of his voice, in the way he narrowed his eyes against the blue shimmers that reflected off the pool, and in the quiet intensity of his gaze as he stood before her.

She felt the tension ease from her a little more.

Jack reached for her hands. His fingers felt warm and strong. She noted how much larger his hands were than hers. And appreciated how gently he'd touched her the night before.

"Paige," he murmured. "Please don't leave. I've wanted you since I was in high school. And I want you even more now. There's never been anyone but you." He looked sincere—even the laugh lines around his eyes seemed worried, waiting for her response. "I...I don't know what I'd do without you."

She swallowed the lump in her throat. She'd spent all

afternoon figuring out what she was going to do without him, but suddenly— "I…I don't want to live without you, either," she answered.

A slow, relieved grin made its way across his lips, and she realized how much she would have missed that smile.

"Does that mean you'll unpack your bags and stay?" he asked.

"Mmm, maybe." She grinned slightly.

He cocked an eyebrow. "Just maybe?"

Her grin widened.

"I think you better stay for sure," he said, "because I saw Irene eyeing me the other day. I think you've got competition."

A low chuckle traveled up Paige's throat. She went to give him a playful shove, but Jack dodged to the side to avoid it.

Instead, he accidentally stepped toward the edge of the swimming pool. His foot slipped, and he waved his arms for balance…and failed.

Before Paige knew it, the owner of the grand resort toppled into his own pool.

Jack resurfaced, laughing. He flipped his wet hair back, droplets fanning in an arc. Treading water, he wiped his face. A wicked gleam sparked in his eyes, and he grinned. "Come on in, the water's warm," he called. He reached out and splashed a perfect wave across the deck at Paige.

She shrieked and hopped backward, but not in time to save the bottom fringe of her sundress. She shook out her wet skirts and glanced at Jack in the pool.

Ghostly reflections danced off the surface of the water, illuminating his handsome face. His eyes darkened and then turned suggestive. "Care to join me?"

His low voice taunted her. A tempting offer when she thought about it. Especially when he looked so inviting. She glanced down at her dress.

"Oh, that's right. A professional student wouldn't want to get all wet," he teased.

She met the challenge in his eyes. She was no longer the bookish academic she'd been when she'd arrived. Being with Jack, she'd learned how to live in the moment, take charge and do what made *her* happy.

Without further thought, Paige answered his dare. She took three running strides and leapt toward Jack, her skirts a rustling whoosh about her legs.

It was a leap into the unknown, a leap toward possibility, a leap for love.

She landed with a splash, the shock of cool water rushing against her flesh.

It was exhilarating.

She surfaced, gasping.

"Wow," he said, admiration evident in his gaze. He lowered his voice to a warning level. "But I'm afraid Irene's not going to like this."

Paige chuckled, her flowing hair dragging beneath the water.

Jack reached for her and drew her against him. Their bodies collided, and suddenly she felt the difference. Something changed between them, becoming more serious, more intense. She stilled in his embrace, and they stared back at each other, inches away, her fingers splayed across his strong shoulders.

"I've never been in love before," he whispered softly. His piercing gaze held her captive. He moved his eyes along her hair and over her face. "If love means life is no longer interesting unless you're a part of it—" his voice became husky "—then I think I'm in love with you."

Her heart skipped a beat.

Jack slid the thin strap of her sundress to the side and pressed a kiss along her wet flesh.

She shivered beneath his touch.

"Maybe I'd been waiting for you to return to the island all these years," he murmured against her skin. "And I didn't even know it."

She smiled.

He moved his hand along her waist, gently stroking. "And maybe you were waiting for me, too?"

"Maybe I was." Her words were breathless, her senses focused on the masculine fingers that dallied beneath the water.

"Just maybe?"

Paige felt his bold fingers tickle along her bare thigh beneath her floating skirt. She sucked in a breath. Expelling it, she asked, "Are you asking if I love you?"

He grinned. "Maybe." The water lapped gently against them.

"Then I love you, too, Jack."

He kissed her softly. "Did I ever tell you that I love it when you call me Jack?"

She pulled back in his arms a bit. "But what if I like the name Jackson?"

He groaned. "Jackson's what my mother calls me when she's irritated."

"Then I'll save it just for scoldings."

His sexy chuckle hovered inches from her mouth. "I do tend to get naughty at times." He moved his hands upward and cupped the curve of her bottom.

She grinned, liking his idea of naughty. She ran her hand along his cheek. His rough stubble tickled beneath her palm. "You need a shave," she murmured.

"Do I? Guess I've had other things on my mind."

"Oh? Like what?"

"Like wondering how to get a certain Ph.D. student to move back to Kauai." He gazed at her. "What do think? Would you consider moving back here? If not, I can move to California so you can continue your classes at Stanford." He paused. "That is, if you'll have me."

"You'd move to California for me?"

"Absolutely."

"But what about Lealea?"

"I can hire someone to manage the resort while I'm away. Or sell the whole chain if necessary."

"But you love Lealea—"

He put a finger against her lips. "Yes, but I love you even more."

Her heart soared, and she swallowed a welling of emotion.

Jack shifted her in his arms, sending gentle waves dancing across the water's surface. "What do you say,

Paige?" he asked softly. "The next time I kiss you, will it be the start of our new life…together?"

She smiled softly and nodded.

He dropped a gentle kiss on her lips.

She returned his kiss with heartfelt sincerity, then pulled back a bit, gazing at the man she loved. "You don't have to do anything drastic like sell this place, though. I love Lealea, just like you do. Besides, I think I have a solution."

"You do?"

"Mmm-hmm. Just like you, I've started a little list of my own."

"You have?"

"Yep. I've been thinking. Number One, opportunities for work and research are immeasurable in Hawaii. I could take courses on Polynesian culture here if I wanted. Or Number Two, I could get a job. Maybe work with birds, help the endangered species of the islands. The options are limitless." She bobbed gently in the pool. "As long as I'm with you, I know I'll be happy." She smoothed a lock of wet hair off his forehead. "I'll move back here, and we'll take things from there, okay?"

"That sounds like a perfect plan." He nuzzled the side of her neck and grinned. "You know, I never thought as a kid back in school that I'd ever have you in my arms like this. But I sure dreamed about it. We've come a long way together, haven't we?"

"We sure have," she murmured. "From Mr Smith's Biology class, to the debate team, to competing for val-edictorian. And now…this."

"I'm glad we're on the same team this time."

"Me, too." Her smile slowly faded. "I have a question, though. I thought you liked being a bachelor." She raised an eyebrow, waiting.

"Sure, I liked it," he agreed. "But that was before I figured out that being fancy-free isn't all it's chalked up to be. Not if it means living without you."

The breath caught in her throat, and she held him close. "Then kiss me," she whispered. "And make it for keeps."

Jack pulled her against him and turned, pressing her back against the side of the pool. He lowered his lips to hers in a fierce, smoldering kiss. Their bodies melded together, gliding intimately beneath the water.

Paige kissed him back with the same heated fervor.

With a low groan, he pulled away, his breathing labored. "Paige," he murmured against her cheek. "Maybe we should move this to my suite. And to a bed this time. Because, if not, in another minute or two I'll be showing you how naughty I can be...right here, in the pool." He proceeded to whisper in her ear an earthy, sensual list of all the things he planned to do with her.

"Mmm, *Jackson*." A slow, languorous smile made its way across her lips. Paige proceeded to reply, in kind, with an equally suggestive list of her own.

As Jack listened he raised his eyebrows in appreciation, and in that moment he swept her into his arms and carried his newly converted list maker out of the pool.

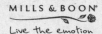

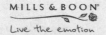

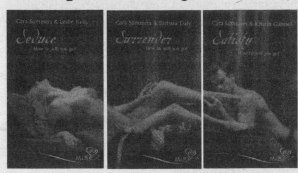